Hearts *racing*.
Blood *pumping*.
Pulses *accelerating*.

*Falling in love can be a blur...
especially at 180 mph!*

So if you crave the thrill of the chase—on and off the track—you'll love

A CHANCE WORTH TAKING
by Carrie Weaver

"I hire the best. You have nothing to worry about, Tess. I'm not going to let anything happen to Michael."

"But it's not all in your hands. There are thousands of variables beyond your control."

"Yes, just like everything else in life. But I don't play fast and loose with my drivers. Your son's in good hands."

"I hope so. Because if I suspect not I'll take him back to Phoenix so fast it'll make your head spin. Don't think I can't or won't. Michael's my world. I'd do anything for him. *Anything.*"

Sam nodded. "That much is obvious. I admire your dedication, even if I think it might be misplaced."

"I'd rather be too cautious than have regrets later."

"Oh, but Tess, what about fun?" His eyes sparkled.

"Fun isn't all it's cracked up to be." She tried not to respond to his charm.

He smiled. "We'll see."

Dear Reader,

In the early stages of creating *A Chance Worth Taking*, I asked my two teenage sons a hypothetical question. If they had to choose between an education at a prestigious university and the chance of becoming a NASCAR driver, which would they choose? My heart skipped a beat when they answered without hesitation—they would choose NASCAR, of course. As a mother who loves books and values learning, I have to admit I'd hoped for a different answer.

In *A Chance Worth Taking*, Tess McIntyre runs into a similar challenge when her near-genius son, Michael, throws away a scholarship at Stanford to follow his dream of becoming a NASCAR driver. And she's none too pleased with Sam Kincaid, owner of the Kincaid Racing Team, for giving Michael the opportunity.

Tess's story is one of learning to let go. And in letting go, she opens herself up to receiving so much more than she ever dreamed.

Thank you for accompanying her on this journey.

Yours in reading,
Carrie Weaver
www.carrieweaver.com

P.S. I enjoy hearing from readers via my Web site or by snail mail at P.O. Box 6045, Chandler, AZ 85246-6045.

//////// NASCAR®

A CHANCE WORTH TAKING

Carrie Weaver

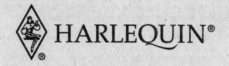

HARLEQUIN®

TORONTO • NEW YORK • LONDON
AMSTERDAM • PARIS • SYDNEY • HAMBURG
STOCKHOLM • ATHENS • TOKYO • MILAN • MADRID
PRAGUE • WARSAW • BUDAPEST • AUCKLAND

ISBN-13: 978-0-373-21780-9
ISBN-10:   0-373-21780-3

A CHANCE WORTH TAKING

CARRIE WEAVER

With two teenage sons, two dogs and three cats, Carrie Weaver often feels she lives in a state of choreographed chaos. Her books reflect real life and real love, with all the ups, downs and emotion involved.

This book is dedicated to Michael. You are my sunshine.

ACKNOWLEDGMENT

I'd like to thank the following people:

Anthony Ruddy for sharing his experiences
and explaining how it feels to race a stock car.

Jamie Rodway at Roush Racing
for arranging our tour of the Roush facilities and
entertaining us at lunch with racing stories.

Emily Ross at NASCAR for sharing her technical expertise.

As always, any inconsistencies in translating
the real world to a fictional world are strictly mine.

PROLOGUE

Tess McIntyre's hand trembled as she gave the envelope to Michael. "It's thick. That's a good sign."

"Uh-huh. Usually." He accepted the envelope, eyeing the return address. "Stanford."

"Of course it's Stanford. The one we've been waiting for."

He took his time opening the envelope. She almost snatched it away to rip it open herself. Then she detected the sparkle in his eyes.

"You're teasing me."

His crooked grin warmed her heart, even while she wanted to wring his neck. It had always been that way. Her precious, precocious son.

"You make it too easy, Mom. You're so transparent. I don't know who wants this more—me or you."

"I only want what's best for you. A top-notch school will open so many doors for you."

Doors I didn't have available. But she didn't voice the thought. She never wanted to make Michael feel guilty.

"Dad didn't get a college degree."

"He had a few college credits. And apprenticed with

a very talented ironworker. You'll be studying physics. You can't even get your foot in the door without at least a master's degree."

"You know I haven't decided on a major."

"Plenty of time for that later. The first year, you'll just be getting core classes out of the way."

He sighed heavily.

She reached out and brushed the hair off his forehead, just as she'd done when he was a little boy. But he wasn't a boy anymore. At eighteen, he was technically a man.

"What does the letter say?"

He removed the thick packet from the envelope and slowly unfolded the pages. This time, he wasn't delaying to tease her. His frown hinted at something else. Fear of failing? Fear of success?

"Whatever it says, I love you. Community college or Stanford, you're still my baby."

He glanced up to meet her gaze. "I know, Mom. But you'd prefer Stanford."

"Okay, I admit it. Read."

She watched his expression carefully as he scanned the page.

His smile was guarded when he said, "I've been offered a full ride."

Tess squealed, then grasped his shoulders and pulled him into a bear hug. "You did it!"

"Yeah, I did."

"Aren't you happy? This is such an accomplishment. And so much more than I could afford for you. You did it all on your own."

His smile was slow. "Yeah, me and my genius brain cells. Good thing you and Dad were better at creating progeny than staying married."

Tess's smile faltered.

"I'm sorry, Mom. I didn't mean it the way it sounded."

She patted his arm. "I know you didn't." She quickly changed the subject. "We'll have to request a Stanford catalog and start plotting your course load."

"Yeah. Sounds great."

Tess closed her eyes in bliss. "It'll be hard having you in California, but it'll be worth it. You can fly home on long holidays."

She opened her eyes. "May I see the letter?"

He handed the papers to her.

"It says here there's an orientation coming up in two months. I'll need to request vacation time. We can drive, just the two of us. It'll be fun."

"Sure. Fun."

Tess refused to be disappointed by his lukewarm response. Once he realized what a tremendous opportunity this was, he'd be more enthusiastic.

CHAPTER ONE

TESS ARRIVED HOME from work dog tired but excited. A big case at work had settled out of court, her boss had promised her a raise and she was headed to California for the weekend.

Her good mood evaporated the moment she walked through the door. Instead of waiting expectantly, duffel bag by the door, Michael was lying on the couch, remote in hand, TV blaring.

"Are you all packed?" She forced cheer into her voice. "We'll need to leave as soon as rush hour dies down."

He sat up. "Mom, we need to talk."

She didn't like those words any more than she'd liked them fifteen years ago when Michael's father had said virtually the same thing.

"What is it?"

"I don't want to go to Stanford."

Tess mentally checked the calendar. Nope, it was July. April Fools' Day was already past.

"You're probably just getting nervous. It's understandable. By Thanksgiving, Stanford will seem like a second home."

"It's not that…. Josh at the driving school said I have real talent."

She sat on the couch next to him. "I'm sure you do, honey. Lots of people do."

"I can make it to the big time—I know it."

"You're already in the big time. It's not many boys who earn full scholarships to Stanford. Fewer still who are as talented in science as you." She reached out and grasped his hand. "You're an extremely lucky kid. The sky will literally be your limit. You'll be able to go places, see things, make huge contributions to the world."

He glanced away. "That all sounds really good, Mom." His voice lacked the passion she'd anticipated.

"Michael, talk to me. What's going on?"

"I'm grateful for all you've done for me…"

"What any mother would do."

He shook his head. "No, it's more. You've always been there for me. Encouraging me, helping me. Working like crazy to make sure I could go to a prep school."

"Hey, you passed me up in math by the time you were in fourth grade. I had to find staff I knew would challenge you."

"And before that, when I was in public school, you made sure they tested me for the gifted program, even though my teachers just thought I was a smart-aleck kid who couldn't sit still."

"They didn't understand you. Your thought processes were so advanced."

He grinned. "Yeah, I guess it would be kind of hard. I didn't get it, though. I felt like a freak."

She cradled his chin with her hand. "You were *never* a freak."

"Well, anyway, thanks for going to bat for me all those times. I'm sure it wasn't easy."

Tess felt the weight of those years on her shoulders. Always struggling to provide the best environment for her son, while making a living as a paralegal. But it had been worthwhile. Michael would get his education and soar. As corny as it sounded she was merely the wind beneath his wings.

And what would she do when her baby flew the nest? Tess pushed away the disturbing thought. She'd deal with that when the time came.

"Michael, you've been an absolute joy and I don't regret a second of it."

"Not even the time I almost blew up the science lab?"

Her heart beat faster as she recalled receiving that phone call from the school. But she managed to smile, as if it hadn't given her a few gray hairs. "So you took out a couple desks and singed off your eyebrows? No permanent damage."

"You're making this hard, Mom."

"Making what hard? Are you worried about being so far from home? Because it's only an hour by plane."

"I'm trying to tell you something."

"So tell me."

"I have, but you haven't been listening. I've made up my mind. I'm *not* going to Stanford."

"Of course you are. We—I mean you—have worked so hard for this."

"I'm not going to college at all."

Tess shot to her feet. "Michael Royce McIntyre—"

"I know education means a lot to you, but I don't need a diploma for what I want to do."

"Look, going out of state is a little scary. Give Stanford a try. If it doesn't work out, you can transfer to Arizona State."

"You just don't get it. I want to be a NASCAR driver."

His level stare kept her from laughing. Kept her from even breaking a smile. Michael had always been such a purposeful child. He didn't do anything on a whim.

She sighed. "You've given this a lot of thought, haven't you?"

"Yes."

She didn't know which disappointed her more. That her child was intent on throwing away his future. Or that he'd done some serious decision-making without asking her opinion.

She tried to summon the strength and common sense to handle this development. Grasping his hand, she said, "I know you enjoy your driving lessons. Despite my initial reservations, you seem to have really taken to that kind of thing."

She mentally cursed her ex-husband and his inability to act like a responsible adult. He'd given Michael driving lessons at the Boyd School of Performance Driving for his sixteenth birthday. In her opinion, it had been an extravagant, wildly impractical gift. Typical Royce.

"I've been trying to tell you for months how much I

want this. It feels like the right thing to do. But you're so intent on Stanford, you just won't listen to anything else."

Tess swallowed hard. Her voice was soft when she said, "I'm listening now."

He leaned forward. "School is great. Science is great. But when I'm driving a race car, it's like flying. Like everything else just fades away. It's me and the car and my brain just goes in fifty million directions."

"I've heard there can be…an adrenaline rush."

"It's more than that. It's almost like, um, a religious experience."

Oh, boy. What could she say to that? All she wanted to do was grab her precious son by the shirtfront and shake some sense into him.

Taking a deep breath, she said, "You've always been levelheaded. I've never had to worry about you getting mixed up in the stuff other kids get into—shoplifting, vandalism, ditching school. Or worse."

"That you know of." The glint of mischief in his eyes was almost her undoing.

"I'm not going to ask what that means. What I'm saying is that I respect your opinion. Tell me what your plans are, and we can approach it logically."

"You mean so you can talk me out of it. But it's not going to happen."

When had he gotten so smart? He'd always been near genius, but this was something altogether different. Stubborn independence without thought to consequences. But part of her applauded him. She'd always secretly worried that his attitudes made him old before his time.

Lord, this was difficult.

"Of course I'll try to talk you out of it. I truly believe education is the key to having a good life. Once you have that degree, nobody can take it away from you. Nobody can deny you opportunities simply because you don't have that piece of paper."

"I know. I've heard this lecture a million times."

"I've always tried to be fair with you, even when we didn't agree. Now will be no different."

"Whew, I was afraid you'd lock me in my room till I was thirty."

Tess cleared her throat. "Tell me what Josh said."

"He thinks I have talent. Says he's never seen anything like it. I'm a natural. Plus I can calculate the physics of a track and variables like wind and temperature and process it to know exactly how the car will respond and—"

"Whoa." She raised a hand, laughing. "So your argument is that you can quit school because you'll be using physics as a race-car driver?"

"Um, yeah. And make a ton of money. I'll buy you a house on the beach in California. You won't have to work again."

She smiled. "You're a sweet boy. I like to work. Besides, you have a greater chance of being struck by lightning than becoming a NASCAR driver."

"Aren't you the one who told me I could be whatever I wanted to be? Not to listen to anyone who said I couldn't do something?"

"Yes, but that wasn't supposed to apply to your mother." She grinned wryly. "I bet you'd make a crackerjack attorney."

"Josh said he'd call a few people he knows in NASCAR and tell them about me."

Tess raised her hand to stop any more plans. "I'll make you a deal. We'll look into the NASCAR thing if you continue getting ready for Stanford. Then, when we have all our facts, we'll discuss it further."

She meant when he found out he didn't have a snowball's chance in hell of becoming a NASCAR driver, he wouldn't have forfeited his spot at Stanford. And ruined his future in the process. But she didn't want to be the one to dash his dreams.

His eyes narrowed. "You don't think I can do it. But I will. You'll see."

Tess's heart sank at the new maturity in his gaze. The way his jaw tightened. Somehow, her son had become a man when she wasn't looking.

SAM WALKED UP the concrete drive to the McIntyre home, noting the neat lawn and the proliferation of blooming plants. Bougainvillea, hibiscus and several other varieties he couldn't name. Probably hybrids bred to withstand the heat of Arizona.

He broke a sweat just walking from the air-conditioned car to the front door. He knocked, hoping they would let him in quickly. A guy could melt in the triple-digit heat. But the kid was worth it; he could feel it in his bones.

Michael McIntyre opened the door. "Mr. Kincaid."

He offered his hand, his grasp firm and sure. Sam's estimation of the boy rose another notch, if that was possible.

"Please come in."

Sam stepped into a homey yet elegant front room.

"Have a seat." Michael walked through an archway and called, "Mom, someone here to see you."

Sam thought it was a strange way to announce him. But then again, most everything his kids had done at the same age had seemed strange. Shrugging, he figured it was just an awkward stage. They'd work on Michael's social skills.

A brunette entered the room. She glanced at him inquiringly.

He rose, extending his hand. "I'm Sam Kincaid."

She took his hand briefly and let it drop. "I'm sorry, Mr. Kincaid, whatever you're selling, I'm not interested."

Michael cleared his throat. "Mom, he has an appointment. To discuss racing."

The woman stopped in her tracks. "I'm sorry, I don't understand…."

Sam pulled a business card from his breast pocket and handed it to her. "I'm here to discuss the possibility of adding Michael to my team."

"Team?"

Poor kid, the genius genes obviously hadn't come from his mother. She seemed a few bricks shy of a full load.

"Yes, the Kincaid Racing team. We're relatively new, but hope to have drivers in serious contention for the NASCAR NEXTEL Cup within the next couple years."

Her eyes widened, and the color drained from her face. "NASCAR? NEXTEL?"

"Surely Michael discussed this with you?"

"I did. A couple weeks ago." But the boy wouldn't meet his eyes.

"You said this evening would be fine with your mother."

Michael's chin came up a notch. "It's as good a time as any."

"Mrs. McIntyre, I'm very sorry. I wouldn't drop in unannounced. I was under the impression you were apprised of my interest in Michael."

"I haven't been apprised of anything." She turned to her son and crossed her arms over her chest. "What's the meaning of this?"

"I didn't think you'd meet with him if you knew ahead of time."

Sam winced. He'd stepped into the middle of a family mess. "This is a new situation for me. Though technically Michael's an adult, because he's only eighteen, I wanted to meet with his parents. Apparently Mr. McIntyre is out of the country?"

"Yes, his father's working in Russia." Her eyes narrowed. "Michael's education comes first and foremost. How do you plan to accommodate that?"

It was Sam's turn to feel left out of the loop. "There will be extensive training involved."

"I'm talking about Stanford. Michael has a full scholarship."

Oh, man, it was worse than he'd thought. Reassuring her with safety statistics was a given. Convincing her it was a good thing the kid wanted to throw away a free ride at a prestigious university was another.

"He…neglected to mention that."

"Michael Royce McIntyre, what is the meaning of this? It sounds as if you've been playing both ends against the middle."

"Look, I should have told you. But I know how bad you want me to go to Stanford and I didn't think you'd listen to Mr. Kincaid."

"You were absolutely right." She turned to Sam. "I'm sorry you made the trip for nothing. I can't condone my son tossing aside a priceless education to drive around in circles. Goodbye."

"There's a lot more to it than that. Have you seen Michael drive?"

"I tried. But I can't." She glanced away. "It scares me to watch."

Ah. Fear he could understand, had even anticipated. "NASCAR takes safety very seriously. Stock-car racing at this level is one of the safest sports around. They've made great strides in protecting the driver."

She raised her chin. "Be that as it may, I want Michael to complete his education. That's something no one can ever take away from him."

"With all due respect, a college diploma doesn't ensure success or happiness."

"It doesn't hurt." Her tart response made him smile in grudging admiration.

"I don't have a college degree and I've done pretty well." Or at least that's what his bottom line indicated. He hadn't always thought that way, though. Once, he'd desperately wanted to attend college.

"I don't intend to debate the point with you. I cannot,

in good conscience, give my blessing to this plan of Michael's. And as a responsible adult, I don't see how you can, either."

"I'm very responsible, Ms. McIntyre. But I believe in dreams, too. And I think Michael deserves this shot. With the right training, he has a darn good chance at making it big."

CHAPTER TWO

SAM KINCAID SPOKE of dreams. But divorce had ruined Tess's dreams. Dreams of a white picket fence, 2.5 children and "till death do us part." Could she have denied Royce his dreams to save her marriage? No. But her son had paid for their mistakes on birthdays and graduations. And every single day when he'd watched his friends' fathers come home from work.

Tess moved to the door, opening it. "I think you should leave, Mr. Kincaid."

The man stayed as if rooted to the spot.

Michael approached, gently removing her hand from the knob and closing the door. "No, he shouldn't. I invited him here because I value your opinion. I'd like you to set aside your prejudices long enough to help me evaluate his offer. I intend to do this. If not with Kincaid Racing, then with someone else. I want you to help me choose the best possible place to start my racing career."

For her quiet son, it was quite a speech. Her stomach knotted when she realized he was absolutely serious and would not be swayed.

She blinked back moisture, trying to get a handle on her disappointment. It wasn't the end of the world. She could still persuade him to change his mind. She just needed to get all the facts, do some research, prepare a logical argument….

"Michael?" The pleading in her voice made her wince.

He touched her shoulder. "Listen to him, Mom. If he's not offering a good deal, we'll go to someone else."

"I assure you, I'm prepared to offer excellent terms. Talented though you are, you're still very young and inexperienced. You haven't even raced much on the local level."

"Raced *much?*" Tess felt the blood drain from her face.

"Yeah, um, I spent a couple Saturday nights out at the track."

"And where did you tell me you went those nights?"

Michael glanced down at his feet, reminding her of when he'd been caught telling a fib as a kindergartner. "The library, spending the night at Ryan's, stuff like that."

"I can't believe you went behind my back." She drew in a shaky breath. "It's a huge betrayal of my trust."

"Only as a last resort. If I'd asked, you would have said no. And since I'm eighteen, I didn't need a parent's permission. I wanted to find out what it felt like to compete, thinking maybe I could figure out one way or the other what I really wanted to do."

"Obviously, you did."

"It just feels so right, Mom. Haven't you ever experienced that?"

Yes, she had. And Michael had been the result. But

she'd never, *ever* felt he was a mistake. That didn't stop her from daydreaming from time to time about the choices she might have made if things had been different. "I think I understand what you're talking about. But what may feel right at the moment could be entirely wrong next week, next month, next year."

"I *have* to try. Or I'll always wonder."

Tess wanted her son to have the choices she'd never had. But *racing?* She hadn't seen that one coming.

As if sensing her weakening, Michael continued, "And with you watching my back on the contract stuff, maybe I can set aside some money for an emergency fund. A backup plan in case it doesn't work out. Enough for college."

Michael was saying all the right things. After all, he knew Tess better than anyone.

"I guess it won't hurt to listen." She moved into the room, sitting on a ladder-back chair. She forced herself to look on this as any other negotiation, thankful for her legal background. "Mr. Kincaid, you said you were prepared to offer generous terms. That means you must see something extraordinary in my son. Chances are, when the other teams find out about his abilities, he'll receive many offers."

Sam shrugged. "Maybe, maybe not. Tell you what, I'll borrow a car for him to run this weekend at Canyon Lake. Seeing him race with a bigger, more experienced crowd ought to tell us something."

Hesitating, she stalled for time. "You can simply borrow a race car?"

Grinning, he said, "Yes, I've got a few local connections. Look at it this way—the kid might freeze or show absolutely no talent when there's serious competition. Then he'd be free to go gangbusters at Stanford. At least he'll know for sure."

Michael remained quiet.

"But you don't think that's going to happen?"

"No, I don't. I've watched him drive. I've observed his intelligence and spirit. I'd bet my reputation he's a winner."

Tess sucked in a breath. Sam Kincaid seemed like a very determined man. "Thank you for being honest. And I'll be just as honest with you. I don't appreciate being put in this position. You've made it very difficult for me to say no."

"Exactly." His eyes sparkled with humor. "I play to win."

"So do I, Mr. Kincaid. So do I."

THE METAL BLEACHER reverberated beneath Tess's rear with every footfall as people streamed up the steps to find a seat. She craned her neck, trying to see Michael's car.

"I brought binoculars if you'd like to use them." Sam stood at the entrance to the row.

Tess reluctantly scooted over. He sat next to her. Spending time with Sam Kincaid wasn't her idea of a relaxing Saturday night. It was more a necessary evil.

"Thank you." She accepted the binoculars. Focusing the lenses, she found Michael's car. He was already inside. At least she assumed it was Michael—with the full-face helmet it was hard to tell.

"I still think I should be down there in the pit area. Is he nervous?" Tess asked.

"Sure. I'd worry if he wasn't. He needs to focus on what he's doing right now. You'd only be another distraction."

She glared at him. "As you've pointed out, Michael's young. He needs to know I'm there for him."

"Oh, I guarantee he knows that." Sam's dry tone grated on her nerves.

"If you have something to say, say it."

He opened his mouth, then shut it. His smile was forced. "Nothing, nothing at all."

She glanced at him, trying to figure the man out. He contained a leashed energy that seemed to beam down toward the track. He tapped the program against his palm.

"You don't have to babysit me, if you need to be in the pits."

He raised an eyebrow. "I think I'm needed more up here."

"You don't have to act like I'm some kind of overbearing mother type. I won't go running down there the minute your back is turned."

"Fair enough. But I'd rather be here. Josh and the guys will do fine."

"Liar."

He grinned, running a hand through his salt-and-pepper hair. "Yeah. And apparently not a very good one."

"So why'd you bring me if you were afraid I'd get in the way?"

"Because Michael is a kid. He's green, he's young and he needs your support. I intend to see that he has it."

"Michael *always* has my support."

"He's never defied you before in a big way, though, has he?"

She hesitated. He'd zeroed in on a sore spot. "No, he hasn't. He's normally very levelheaded."

"He still is. And that will make him a great driver. But he's also growing into a man who wants to go for the brass ring. You gave him that confidence."

"Flattery won't work on me."

He shrugged. "I had to try. What will work?"

"Show me that racing is the best way for my son to have a normal, happy, successful life."

"Guess it depends on your definition of normal."

"Exactly. I've done some online research. NASCAR drivers barely have time at home during the season. They're on the road most weeks."

"Yes."

"How will he have a normal family life? Or will he be like most adrenaline junkies and leave the tough stuff to his wife?"

"That's a huge generalization."

She shrugged, suspecting she was being unfair, but not caring. "It's not hard to figure out."

"Many families fly out to the track every weekend. There's a support infrastructure so they can have as regular a family life as possible. Child care, church services, tutors. You name it. Besides, he's still a young enough guy I doubt he's thinking of settling down yet."

Tess inclined her head. Sam had touched on another of her hot spots. Hadn't she been the one to advise Michael not to get seriously involved until he was out of college and established in his career? Another pearl of wisdom she'd learned the hard way.

But he could be single with a doctorate degree just as easily as he could be a single race-car driver. So she presented one of the many arguments she'd accumulated. "It's life in a fishbowl during the season. If he makes it to competing for the NASCAR NEXTEL Cup, my son will have no privacy to speak of. And you think he's ready for this kind of pressure?"

"I'll make sure he's ready. I promise I won't just throw him out there."

"And how do you propose to do that?"

"Simulators, visualization, practice, practice, practice. Then we'll have him run some amateur races. That's why it's important we start right away if we want him to run in the Busch Series in February. I'll need a decision from Michael by the end of next week."

Tess drew in a deep breath. "This is moving way too fast. You're not giving us time to make a rational decision."

"I'm giving all the time you need. When a kid is as gifted as Michael is, it shouldn't be a difficult choice. Most would feel it's a no-brainer. A once-in-a-lifetime opportunity."

Her mouth dropped open in amazement. "Surely you're not saying choosing a sport over an education is what most people would do?"

"That's exactly what I'm saying."

Tess raised her chin. "The only thing I agree with in that sentiment is the no-brainer part. Anyone with half a brain would choose an education."

Fortunately, the drivers were announced, distracting Tess from her impulse to deck Sam Kincaid.

She couldn't, *wouldn't* condone choosing some elusive quest for fame and fortune over getting an excellent education and a solid start in life.

But, she had to admit, it gave her a little thrill to hear Michael's name announced over the loudspeaker. And the responding rumble of the engines made her heart thump in time with the idling monsters. She wasn't about to share that piece of information with Sam.

When the green flag went down, Tess half rose, trying to see Michael's car. He lost ground, forced to the back of the pack as one car after another jostled for position. It looked as if Michael was politely allowing the cars to pass him.

Of course she'd stressed the importance of manners as he'd grown up. But somehow, she got the feeling they weren't as necessary on the racetrack.

One look at Sam's frown and she was pretty sure she was right.

"Come on, Michael," she murmured. Clenching her hands into fists, she waited for him to get tired of being pushed around. Raising the binoculars, she realized a closer view wasn't always better.

Turning to Sam, she asked, "Are you just going to sit there? Shouldn't you be calling a time-out or something? They're pushing him around out there."

Sam's lips twitched. "Nope. It's up to him."

"He'll get run over."

He nodded. "Possibly. Or he'll get mad, his competitive instincts will kick in and he'll show us what he's made of."

"I'm not sure I like the sound of that."

"I doubt any mother does."

Another car hit Michael's bumper.

She grasped Sam's arm, her nails digging into flesh. "That guy intentionally hit him. There should be rules."

"There are. But that was only a love tap."

"You've got to be kidding."

"Nope. Just a gentle nudge to get him out of the way."

Tess crossed her arms. "It's barbaric."

Sam grinned. "I take it Michael never played football?"

"No." She recalled his one and only junior football game. He'd gotten the breath knocked out of him after being sacked. She'd pulled him from the game right then and there, never to return, much to the derision of the other parents. She'd overheard one father refer to her as a "helicopter mother."

So she opted for an ambiguous qualifier. "He was a more…cerebral child."

"Watch." Sam pointed toward the track. "Your 'cerebral child' just found his bal—um, his competitive spirit."

She forgot to be offended as she watched Michael's car nudge the car in front of him out of the way. Nodding, she said, "Yes, I see. Just a love tap."

Triumph flared for a moment in Sam's eyes. "Exactly."

If Sam thought he had the deal wrapped up and in the bag, he was sadly mistaken.

Michael passed another car. Then another.

"The kid's a born champion," Sam commented.

Tess watched her son maneuver to the front of the pack. "I've known that all along. You've never seen him in a science competition."

"Once racing takes hold of a man's heart, it never lets go. Michael, with the right coaching, will be the next NASCAR phenom. The question is, will you support him so he can follow his God-given path?"

"What does God have to do with racing?"

"Oh, lady, you've got a lot to learn."

SAM WATCHED TESS as she daintily picked her way through the pit area, tiptoeing through the tools and debris inherent to a small track. He wouldn't have been surprised to see her remove an embroidered hankie from her purse and cover her cute little upturned nose. With her long, graceful neck and expressive dark eyes, she reminded him of Natalie Wood, one of his favorite old-time actresses.

How would Tess react when she saw her son? He'd seen the excitement flash in her eyes during the race. He'd also seen fear and anger. It was a toss-up whether she would castigate or congratulate him. All Sam could do was hold his breath and wait.

Michael jogged over, grinning from ear to ear. He picked up his mother and twirled her around. "Did you see that? I won."

Tess smiled down at her son. The love shining in her

eyes made Sam forget her overprotectiveness for a moment. Anything she did for her son was done out of love. But sometimes people did the totally wrong things for the right reasons. He should know.

"I saw, Michael. I was quite impressed."

The woman seriously needed to lighten up.

"It was awesome. Mr. Kincaid, what did you think?"

He clapped Michael on the back. "I think it'd be a shame if you didn't pursue a career in NASCAR. You've got what it takes, kid."

"Wow. Thanks."

Sam wondered how much time Michael's father spent with him. Michael seemed overwhelmed with male praise. But that could be used to their advantage in training.

"Why don't we go somewhere and hammer out the details? The guys'll take care of everything here."

"You're very sure of yourself, Mr. Kincaid."

Whoops. She was back to calling him Mr. Kincaid again.

"Please, call me Sam." It came out more a challenge than a request. He'd been patient. Now it was time to get things moving. "Why don't we get a bite to eat? We can talk it over."

She hesitated. "It's getting late…."

"I'm doing it, Mom. You can come with us or not, but I'm doing it."

Sam held his breath while Tess held her son's gaze.

An expression flickered over her face. Maybe pain, maybe fear.

Tess cupped Michael's face with her hand. "I'll come.

And I'll try to keep an open mind. That's all I can promise."

Sam released his breath. It was a start.

CHAPTER THREE

TESS PUSHED the rubbery meat around on her plate with her fork. The diner had only one distinction; everything was fried. She had ordered chicken-fried steak and what a mistake that had been.

She listened carefully as Sam outlined the hiring terms for Michael and detailed his plans for the probationary period.

"So you see, either one of us can walk away without penalty in the first four months if we find it's not working."

Nodding, she said, "You've offered him what seems a fair base wage, plus incentives. I'd like to check around a bit and find out what the industry standard is."

"Sure. I think you'll find I'm being very fair."

"I prefer to be careful. I'm sure you understand."

"Yes. This is your son's future we're talking about. Now, he'll be staying in a small condo in Charlotte when he's at home base. When he's on the road, he'll have use of a motor home. I'll hire the drivers for the team hauler and the motor home."

When he's on the road.

Tess's breathing grew shallow at the thought of all

the mistakes Michael might make. All the ways he could be hurt.

The entire course of his life could be changed by one moment of carelessness. And there were people in the world just waiting to prey on a boy without much worldly experience.

Whose fault was that? Tess shook her head to dislodge her ex-husband's voice. He'd accused her once of trying to wrap Michael in cotton, depriving him of the experiences most boys had. Royce didn't seem to understand her need to keep their son safe. Just as he hadn't understood her need to keep *him* safe when they were married. It wasn't easy being the one left behind to imagine all the ways her daring husband could be harmed.

Tess forced herself to focus on the here and now. Forced herself to contemplate letting go. Because Michael had made it plain he intended to go, with or without her blessing. And she didn't want to lose her son by holding on too tightly.

"Say Michael does sign with you. It's bound to be a difficult transition from high-school student to race-car driver. What are your plans for ensuring a smooth transition?"

"I'm not sure I understand."

"What kind of supervision will he have?"

Sam frowned. "I'll be there to give him appropriate guidance. Then there will be his crew chief and the other guys on the team."

"I imagine life on the road can get pretty…wild." Again Tess tried not to think of all the pitfalls awaiting a young guy.

"We all have a vested interest in seeing that Michael is focused on his driving. None of us is going to stand by and watch him walk into a situation he can't handle."

"How can you determine what he can or can't handle? You don't even know him."

"Mom, I don't need anyone to watch over me. I'm an adult, not a kid."

Oh, if only he knew what a long way he had to go.

"I'm trying to reach a solution we can both be comfortable with."

Sam raised his hand to forestall further arguing from Michael. "If it were my son dealing with a total stranger at eighteen, I might be cautious, too. Bottom line, Michael is a born driver and I think I can mold him into a champion. I'll find some way to handle your concerns so we all can be comfortable with this partnership. Maybe Michael can defer his scholarship at Stanford? Then he doesn't risk losing his education if this doesn't work out."

The sincerity in Sam's eyes reassured Tess. She exhaled slowly. "Thank you. I appreciate your understanding."

Snapping his fingers, Sam leaned forward. "I have another idea you might find acceptable, Tess. How about if you serve as his adviser? That way you know he's properly supervised."

"Me? How can I advise him from Phoenix?"

"I meant you would come to Charlotte. I could provide a two-bedroom condo and you'd stay with Michael. Say, for a few months? He should be settled in by then."

"He'll certainly need longer than that to adjust. I have a job. I can't just up and move." But the idea was unbelievably attractive. A new place, new people, and the opportunity to simply guide Michael instead of carrying the whole household on her shoulders. Besides, it might give her boss the opportunity to see how much she did around there. Her recent raise notwithstanding, she'd been there so long he tended to take her for granted.

"See, she can't go," Michael chimed in.

"Could you take a six-month leave of absence? If things go well, you could come back earlier."

"Maybe." Tess wondered if she was as indispensable as her boss led her to believe. "But there would be living expenses."

"I can finagle the budget to give you a small stipend, too." He named a figure.

"Let me think about it over the weekend. If I decide I like the idea, I'll ask about a leave of absence Monday. I should be able to give you an answer Monday afternoon."

"Okay. I'll expect to hear from you then."

TESS STARED at the gray walls of her cubicle and wondered if she should pinch herself. The senior partner at the law firm had granted her leave of absence without a single argument, assuring her the other paralegals would take good care of her cases. The Realtor already had a client who might rent her house. And Sam was making arrangements to have their personal items shipped to Charlotte, where he'd rented furniture for the condo. Her Corolla would go into storage, because Sam had cars he would make available for both of them.

Tess focused on her computer screen. Her hands started to tremble, but it had nothing to do with the personal-injury demand packet she composed. This was huge. The last time she'd had a change this big, she'd run off and married Royce McIntyre right after high-school graduation. The realities of single parenthood had stamped out any desire she might have had to take future risks.

Swallowing hard, she tried to recapture the spark of excitement she'd felt when Sam first proposed the idea. But instead of anticipation, Tess felt anchorless, as if she might simply float away once she didn't have her familiar routine to keep her safe.

Rebecca, one of the paralegals, came by her desk. "I hear you're taking a leave of absence."

"Yes."

"Hey, you get to hang out with all those hunky NASCAR drivers. That's got to be the best leave ever." Her eyes sparkled with anticipation.

"Um, yes, it'll be great." Tess tried to smile brightly, but failed.

"Are you okay?" Rebecca asked.

"Yes, I'm fine. This has just been very…sudden."

"Maybe we'll see Michael on TV."

Not likely. "Maybe."

"Well, take care."

The partners and staff threw her a party on Friday afternoon. Tess felt an odd finality to it, as if she were retiring. But, to be fair, they were merely happy she was to have this adventure, not pushing her out the door.

Or out of the nest, more likely.

She'd come to depend on the routine of her career, any need for variety fulfilled in the wide range of personal-injury cases. The satisfaction of a job well done gave her confidence. Knowing she was a good mother gave her peace. What more did she need?

Tess suspected she was about to find out.

SAM CURSED HIMSELF for being every kind of fool. What initially had seemed like the perfect solution now seemed like a six-month sentence in hell.

He arrived at the airport early, only to hang around the baggage-claim area. Sure, he could have sent one of his guys to pick up Tess and Michael, but somehow it seemed important for him to do it. As if to prove how committed he was to Michael's career. And how reliable.

Heck, he couldn't get much more committed. Unless, of course, the kid had a pet and a girlfriend he wanted to drag to Charlotte, too. And as for being reliable, he doubted Mama Bear Tess would find anyone reliable enough to entrust with her son.

Earning Tess's trust would be tough. Convincing her to let go and get out of Michael's way could be nearly impossible. But he'd never shied away from a challenge and he didn't intend to start now.

He watched closely for Michael and Tess when people started straggling toward the luggage conveyer. Most stared at the rectangular opening with zombielike intensity, as if they could will their luggage to appear.

Then he saw Michael striding toward him. Tess

followed at a more moderate pace. Almost to the point of dragging her feet.

He suppressed a smile. She didn't want to be in this situation any more than he did. At least they agreed on one point.

And the sooner he could calm her motherly fears and send her back to Phoenix, the better.

TESS PULLED her rolling suitcase as she followed Sam from the parking lot toward the block of condos.

"Everything's so green," she murmured.

"A lot different from Phoenix, huh?" He led them to a downstairs apartment. Producing a key, he unlocked the door and handed the key to Tess, then opened the door wide for her to pass.

She entered the condo and didn't know what to say. Her gaze followed the lines of the soaring ceiling and entryway. The exposed wood beams and nail-head-trimmed leather sofas created a homey, casual atmosphere.

"I wasn't able to re-create your own home, but I picked out rental furniture I thought you would be comfortable with. They don't have antiques for obvious reasons."

"It's beautiful," she breathed, trailing her hand over the back of the couch. "I'll scour the flea markets and antique stores. I love sifting through all the junk to find something that strikes a chord. If it needs a little TLC, all the better. I've refinished most of my own pieces myself."

"You did a terrific job, then. I was worried you might find this place lacked the character of your place."

"Oh, but that's the fun of it." She turned and placed her hand on his arm. "Thank you. It's lovely."

"Don't you want to see the rest?"

"Of course. But it's already much more than I expected. When you said a small two-bedroom apartment, I visualized the place my ex-husband and I rented right after we married. Rooms not much bigger than a walk-in closet."

He shrugged. "This place was the most appropriate choice that was available."

"I'm gonna go check out the bedrooms," Michael said.

Tess followed, bemused. She'd been dreading uprooting herself and Michael, worried that she was such a creature of habit she might be homesick. But this place already felt familiar. With a few personal touches, she could visualize settling in.

"This one's mine, Mom." Michael threw his duffel bag on the bed. The nautical theme was unobtrusive, but decidedly masculine. Navy and cream were the predominant colors, with a splash of red here and there.

"I figured the theme would be NASCAR, with black-and-white checkered curtains," she commented.

Sam chuckled. "Nah. It's actually good to have a place to forget about racing, if just for a while. Besides, Michael won't be spending much time here after the initial training."

"Hey, Mom, come here and look at your room."

Tess crossed the hall, with Sam bringing up the rear. She inhaled deeply, savoring the scent of fresh flowers. A vase of mixed flowers was placed in the center of the dresser.

The walls were painted a muted gold, the decor giving her the impression of a Tuscan villa. A painting of a white sand beach and deep-blue ocean completed the effect. It wasn't what she would have chosen, but it touched off a longing deep inside her. She'd always wanted to travel to Italy and the Mediterranean.

Shaking her head, Tess reminded herself she was here for Michael. "It's lovely. I can't wait till our things arrive."

"They should be here Thursday." Sam eyed her intently, as if waiting for her stamp of approval. What more could she say?

"Truly, Sam, it's way more than I expected. Thank you." She wished she could be more effusive, but all she could think of was a warm soak in the tub. "I'm awfully tired and would like to get settled in."

"Of course. I'll bring your luggage from the other room."

"No need to do that."

"Yes, there is. I intend to see that you've got everything you need while you're here."

His attention flustered her. She'd never met a man quite so interested in her comfort. It was something she feared she could get accustomed to.

"How far from the track are we?" Michael asked.

"About twenty minutes."

"Cool. Maybe someday I can learn how to fly and get my own helicopter. Then I can fly to the track every day."

Tess opened her mouth to tell Michael that helicopters were obscenely expensive and probably dangerous, too.

But something held her back. Maybe it was the hope reflected in his eyes, the anticipation of an exciting, fulfilling adventure. A hope she'd lost long ago.

"Always dream big, kid. Always dream big." Sam said it with such confidence, Tess might have agreed with him. If his theory didn't come with such a huge risk attached.

CHAPTER FOUR

THE DAYS FLEW BY as Tess observed Michael and his training. She was pretty sure Sam would have preferred she stay at the condo and watch daytime TV, but Tess was accustomed to being an integral part of her son's life, and this was no different.

She smiled as he spun out and muttered under his breath. In a simulation, it was amusing. On the track, it would have had her biting her nails.

"He's improving," Sam said.

"Yes. He's barely wrecked all day. Which brings me to a question. Surely he's not going to wreck like this on a real track?"

"The simulation is designed for avoiding dangerous situations. To train his brain and muscles to work together, quickly evaluating situations to take the best evasive action. On the track, he doesn't have time to consciously go through a mental checklist. It has to be automatic, split-second."

"I see. And here I thought he was just playing video games."

"No, the simulation is very important. There are other techniques I intend to use that others might find...unusual."

"I don't like the sound of that."

"Nothing wild. I think Michael might benefit from visualization training. Many athletes utilize it."

"Like visualizing himself winning?"

"Something like that. Only more direct. More focused. It will help his confidence."

Nodding, she said, "I imagine it will. I never knew so much went into racing. I mean, I've heard the old Haul Butt And Turn Left adage. As if driving a race car was a gift, not something that could be learned."

"Oh, talent and instinct are a great part of it. But honing Michael's natural abilities will enhance his performance."

"You sound like he's training to be a weight lifter. Which brings me to another question. Is all the fitness training really necessary? The poor boy is stiff and sore every day."

"Top physical fitness is essential. He has to have the stamina to withstand four to six hours inside a hot car. Superior upper-body strength is necessary for steering."

Her head was spinning from all the information she'd received since arriving. She'd never anticipated there would be so much to learn.

"I guess I just never thought of it as a sport like baseball or soccer," she said.

"It's every bit as demanding, if not more so. And the guys don't often get credit for being athletes."

Tess grinned. "My son, an athlete. Who'd have thought? His father will be so proud. All the gifted stuff and academics made Michael's dad a bit uneasy. He's more a man of action."

"You've been divorced long?"

"Since Michael was a toddler."

"I'm sorry. I'm sure being a single parent is very demanding."

She didn't bother to tell him he'd made an incredible understatement. "It is. Do you have children?"

"Yes. A boy and a girl. Grown and on their own."

"Your wife must have shouldered a lot of the day-to-day stuff if you were on the road with NASCAR competitions."

"I wasn't involved in NASCAR back then. I was busy building my real-estate investment firm. And she's my ex now."

"Oh." Tess didn't know what else to say. She was curious to know what went wrong, but too polite to ask.

"The kids were in college when we divorced, so I guess we were fortunate. If any divorce can be considered fortunate."

"Mine certainly wasn't." It had been Royce's decision, not hers—they would still be married if it had been up to Tess. Married, with at least three more kids. But it wasn't meant to be. The loss still made her heart ache at times.

She studied Sam as he watched Michael negotiate a tricky situation on the simulator, one he'd failed several times. Sam grinned when Michael mastered the technique. "He's a great kid. A real go-getter."

"His father's genes, I'm afraid."

Sam raised an eyebrow. "Oh? And what did he get from you?"

"Until a couple months ago, I thought he got his

groundedness, his ability to avoid temptation and move toward a goal."

"And now?"

She shrugged. "Now, I'd guess all he got from me was his hair color."

"You're wrong. He got his persistence, his intelligence, his generous soul from you."

She avoided his eyes. Was that how he really saw her? It was a nice description. "I wasn't very gracious when we first met."

"You were protecting your cub. I'm hoping you'll realize I'm here to help Michael, not hurt him." He hesitated. "Letting go a bit might not be a bad thing."

Tess chuckled. "We were having a moment and you had to go and spoil it. I should have known you had an ulterior motive with all those compliments."

He grinned, accentuating the lines by his eyes. He was a very attractive man. Annoying, but attractive.

"It wasn't BS. But I'll remember not to underestimate you next time."

She raised her chin. "You'd be wise not to underestimate me *any* time. And for the record, I'm not going to up and leave my son in a strange city with people we don't know well."

"He's beginning to settle in."

"I'm not leaving, Sam. You're stuck with me for six months. That was our deal. Better get used to it."

"You're a hard woman."

"I have to be. For my son."

"You're sure about that?"

"Very sure."

But she had to wonder. It hadn't always been that way. For the first two years after Michael had been born, she'd stayed home and nurtured her baby boy. Laughed at his antics, marked his milestones. Loved every minute of being a stay-at-home mom. She'd even enjoyed having dinner in the oven when her husband arrived home from work. Until one day, he arrived home to tell her he was going overseas to make big money for the family.

Even young and naive as she'd been, Tess had been uneasy. Royce hadn't done it *for* the family. He'd done it to get away from the family.

The screech of tires and a curse from Michael drew her out of her reverie. A loud impact followed.

"Michael Royce McIntyre, I don't appreciate that kind of language and I'm sure NASCAR doesn't, either."

Sam nodded. "Your mother's right, Michael."

"Not if nobody hears."

"Son, when you're racing, you've got to figure everyone in the pits will hear what you say. And everyone in the stands tuned in to our frequency and very possibly everyone watching the race on national TV. Don't say anything that can come back to bite you on the rear later."

Michael sighed. "That sucks."

"Michael," Tess warned.

Sam's lips twitched. "Um, yes, it does. Looks like your time at the sim is up. Why don't you go hit the gym?"

Michael stretched. "Sounds good. I've been sitting way too long."

"Better get used to it. Once you're racing, you can expect to be sitting in a hot car for up to six hours."

"No problem. I'll be racing. That'll make the difference."

"Maybe. Maybe not. We'll see."

Tess didn't like the sound of that. Before she could ask Sam to clarify, he said. "I thought we could go tour the garage. Give you an idea of what goes into building a race car."

"I'd like that." Much to her surprise, it sounded interesting. "No matter what my views are on Michael trying to make a career of racing, I appreciate all you've done to help me understand. I'd like you to promise one thing, though."

"What's that?"

"You allow me to return the favor someday. If there's anything I can explain about personal-injury claims, let me know. Though I'm familiar with Arizona laws, not North Carolina."

"Let's hope the need never arises. I wouldn't mind learning how to refinish furniture, though, if you're ever of a mind to teach me."

"Absolutely." Tess smiled, pleased there was some way she could repay him. "There's something really satisfying in finding a piece most people would pass by and making it beautiful again. It's addicting, at least to me."

Sam chuckled. "I wouldn't go that far. But I've got some of my folks' stuff in the attic I might want to refinish. My daughter is always complaining my place looks like a high-end hotel room."

"Ouch."

"Oh, said in the most loving way, mind you. She thinks it needs a woman's touch."

Tess raised an eyebrow. "Trying to get you back together with your ex?"

"Hardly. My ex is happily remarried. More like one of the blissfully-in-love types who wants everyone else to find the same kind of happiness."

She detected a trace of wistfulness in Sam's voice. He covered with a cocky grin.

"So if I fix up the place, give it some personality, maybe she'll get off my back."

"You know, it's very easy to pick up a few key accent items to make a room feel homey." Tess hesitated. "As a matter of fact, I'm going to check out the local flea markets and antique stores Saturday. Want to come?"

She braced herself for tactful backpedaling.

Instead, he said, "Sure. Why not?"

His easy acceptance left her oddly restless. Most of the men she knew would rather have a root canal than go antiquing. "It may not be as exciting as racing."

He tilted his head. "Everything doesn't have to be about racing. Sometimes it's good to experience new things."

"Yes, it is." A strange admission since she'd done her best to avoid change in the past decade or so. Maybe it wasn't change that bothered her as much as risk. It was an idea she intended to mull over later.

"Come on, let's go," Sam said.

The garage wasn't a far walk and Sam entertained her with anecdotes on the way. He seemed to be a man at home in any situation. For some reason, that put her at ease.

They entered the large industrial-looking room.

Tess glanced around. "It's not what I expected. Very clean."

"Always. You expected oil on the floor, with a bunch of grubby guys scratching and spitting?"

She raised an eyebrow. "As a matter of fact, I did."

"We run a top-notch shop. I buy the best equipment and hire the best technicians. With upward of a hundred and seventy thousand dollars in each car, it doesn't pay in the long run to cut corners. We'll start in the chassis-assembly area."

They walked through an arch to where technicians welded the car frame together.

"Michael's father would love this—he's a welder. He started on oil rigs, but works in the mines now."

"Then you ought to know it's a difficult craft to master. One weak weld could compromise the stability of a car."

Tess swallowed hard. Her worries about Michael racing came back in a rush. And not all of them were about losing an education.

"Tess…" The understanding in his brown eyes caught her off guard. "I hire the best. You have nothing to worry about. I'm not going to let anything happen to Michael."

"But it's not all in your hands. There are thousands of variables beyond your control."

"Yes, just like everything else in life. I don't play fast and loose with my drivers—we take safety seriously. Your son's in good hands."

"I'd like to believe you, Sam. I *have* to believe you if I'm to sit back and watch my son drive 180 miles per hour on a track with forty-two other cars."

"Good. We'll think positively and train Michael to be the best, safest driver out there."

"The two aren't mutually exclusive?"

"Not at all. Like any sport, playing smart is the best way to win. It's also the best way to stay safe."

She held his gaze. "I hope so. Because if I suspect my son's being put in harm's way, I'll take him back to Phoenix so fast it'll make your head spin. Don't think I can't or won't."

"I'd never make that mistake. Looks like I've failed miserably at reassuring you."

Shrugging, she said, "I may be a tougher sell than most. Michael's my world. I'd do anything for him. *Anything.*"

Sam nodded. "That much is obvious. I admire your dedication, even if I think it might be misplaced."

"I'd rather be too cautious than have regrets later."

"Oh, but Tess, what about fun?" His eyes sparkled.

"Fun isn't all it's cracked up to be." She tried not to respond to his charm.

He smiled. "We'll see."

SAM WATCHED Tess bargain with the antique store manager. The poor guy didn't stand a chance. She was good, really good.

But then again, he already knew that. A newbie to the racing biz, she'd still hammered out a damn good deal for Michael.

After she paid the manager about half what he'd been asking for the rocker, she turned. A smile lit her face.

He sucked in a breath. She was a beautiful woman. He'd never fully realized the fact, distracted as he was by her *über*-mom role.

"This rocker will be the perfect piece to teach you about refinishing. When it's done, it will be perfect for my great room. Then you ought to be able to tackle some of the stuff in your attic."

He eyed it skeptically. It was painted a horrible shade of light green. "If you say so."

"I know so. Here, try it out."

"I'll take your word for it."

"Try it." Her voice brooked no argument.

He sat, rocking experimentally. "Hey, this isn't bad."

"Give it a minute."

He did. He relaxed in spite of himself. "This has got terrific lumbar support."

Tess trailed her hand along the arm of the chair. "True craftsmanship went into this piece. Once we strip away the layers of paint and refinish it, you'll be totally amazed."

Sam watched her fingers in fascination. Her love of the workmanship came through loud and clear. So clear, in fact, it was almost sensual.

He stood. "Are they going to wrap it or something so it doesn't get damaged?"

"Yes. Do you mind bringing it with us?"

"No." He'd be downright ecstatic to load the darn thing as long as work chased away the images of Tess caressing the chair, which in turn inspired images of Tess caressing him.

Tess tilted her head. "We can come back for the rocker if you'd like. There are still several stores we haven't been in."

"I'd swear we've hit every single one."

She raised an eyebrow. "Surely you're not tired?"

"Of course not." He'd rather die than admit his feet hurt, his back ached and he was starving. "Lead on."

She did, plowing through one antique shop after another. Her purchases were few. But he could spot the quality in each. That was the thing that had stood out to him from the start about Tess. She was one classy lady. Not in the society kind of way. More in innate style and confidence.

Nearly an hour later, she uttered the words he'd been longing to hear. "Let's get lunch."

"I thought you'd never ask."

She grinned. "I know. You've been a good sport, though."

"You've been tormenting me on purpose?"

"*Tormenting* is a bit harsh. I prefer to think of it as testing your dedication. You said stamina was essential in a driver. It's also essential in many other areas of life."

Sam's mind took an R-rated detour and he did a double take.

Her cheeks grew pink. "Not like that."

"Like what?" He couldn't help teasing her.

"I meant, studying and preparing for the world."

"Ah, we're back to square one. And here I thought we were getting past that."

"I won't be past it until you convince me your program is the best thing for my son."

"Has anyone ever told you you're like a pit bull terrier?"

"More than once. I find it complimentary."

He shook his head and laughed. "Of course you do."

"Am I allowed to compare you to an animal now? Turnabout's fair play?"

"How can I say no?"

"You can't."

"Just stick to the vertebrates, okay?"

"Darn, that leaves out my vast repertoire of attorney jokes. I've heard them all." Her eyes sparkled.

"I'm sure you have. Someday you'll have to entertain me with them."

"Maybe. In the meantime, I see you as a mustang."

"The horse, not the car?"

"Yes, the horse. Independent, persevering and noble."

For the first time in a very long time, Sam was rendered speechless. Because he didn't want to mess up this moment. He suspected the fall from noble mustang to something that slithered might be a hard fall indeed.

CHAPTER FIVE

SAM HAD several reasons for choosing Watkins Glen to introduce Michael—and Tess—to the NASCAR Busch Series. One, it was a track where there was room to pass—no need to make Tess nervous with a bump-and-run track like Martinsville. And two, Seneca Lake was a gorgeous place to be in August.

He took her to the pits first, where he found his best crew chief conferring with a driver who was running into a bad stretch.

When he finished, Sam stepped forward. "Ron Waltham, I want you to meet Michael McIntyre and his mother, Tess."

Ron nodded to Tess and shook Michael's hand. "Nice to meet you. Heard some good things about you."

"Wow, and I know all about you. You helped Sonny James turn around his career."

"Sonny did the hard part. I just made a few suggestions."

Sam knew Ron was being too modest. It was one of the things he admired about the man. Ron's only agenda was seeing that his driver won with his integrity intact.

"I'm going to leave Michael in your capable hands.

He'll stay out of your way, but I want him to get a feel for what it's like in the pits during a race of this caliber."

Ron didn't miss a beat. "Sure thing. I'll show him around a bit, then when it gets close to race time, he can shadow the behind-the-wall team."

Sam smiled at Michael's obvious delight. If he wasn't mistaken, the kid was already halfway to hero worship. Not a bad trait in a driver/crew-chief relationship. When even the most experienced driver refused guidance, it was a sure sign of trouble.

Sam clapped Michael on the shoulder. "You'll be in good hands. I'm going to take your mom to my track suite. We'll come find you down here after the race."

Michael nodded, but his attention was already focused on Ron and the stats he pored over.

"'Bye, honey," Tess said.

Sam was grateful the kid wasn't paying attention. He suspected Michael would get some good-natured ribbing from the guys about Tess's apron strings.

"He can't hear you. He's already in another dimension."

"He can be very…focused."

"I know you wish he was less focused on racing, but his passion is a good thing. As long as we can channel it effectively."

Tess shrugged. "I can't help wishing he was that focused on graduating from college."

"He is what he is. We frequently don't choose our passions—they choose us." The certainty of his words reverberated in the air between them.

Tess was silent as they walked to the suite. Finally,

she asked, "You know a little something about conflicting priorities?"

"I've had to make some difficult decisions. Choices that altered the course of my life."

"Were they good decisions?"

He took his time answering. "Some choices are neither good nor bad, just the best we could do at the time."

"That's very cryptic."

He grinned. "Yes, it is. And I intend to keep it that way."

She returned his smile. "What a nice way of telling me to mind my own business."

Shrugging, he guided her toward the buffet table. "I hope you're hungry."

Her eyes widened. "Not *that* hungry. You've got enough food here to feed a family of four for a week."

"Before you say something about how decadent it is when there are children starving, the caterer takes any leftovers directly to a nearby homeless shelter if local regulations allow."

"I guess I don't feel quite so decadent, then."

"Good." He handed her a plate. "Because I, for one, don't intend to hold back. I'll have to impress you another way."

She laughed, a throaty sound that surprised him. Mostly because he could imagine hearing that chuckle in a more intimate context.

Whoa. Put on the brakes, Kincaid. Tess McIntyre was off-limits for reasons too obvious to list. But what better way to distract her from mothering Michael right out of the running?

Tess was beautiful, classy and acted as if she needed someone to show her how to loosen up. Sam reminded himself he definitely wasn't the man for the job.

"Sam, are you okay?" Her voice was warm with concern, doing absolutely nothing to redirect his wandering thoughts.

"Sure. Just thinking of some stats I need to go over."

"I don't want to keep you from important business."

He forced himself to focus on the task at hand. Showing Tess the intricacies of stock-car racing—without thinking of getting involved with her.

"You're not keeping me from anything." He gestured toward the bar. "May I get you a drink while you help yourself to the food?"

"A diet soda would be great."

"Coming right up."

She glanced around. "Are we the only ones here tonight?"

"No, I believe we gave tickets to a few of the sponsors. And my PR team will be here." He hoped they showed up soon. That way he wouldn't be tempted to step over the line with Tess.

They selected seats with the best view of the track, though every view was fantastic from the suite.

Tess balanced her plate on her knee with grace. "Tell me, what's next for Michael?"

"We're going to start hitting the regional tracks pretty hard. Kind of like racing boot camp, until he's so immersed in competition, moving up to the NASCAR Busch Series will be a piece of cake."

"Surely, it's not that easy."

"No, it's not. But we won't tell him that. Confidence in the early stages will get him through some tough adjustments."

"He's never lacked confidence where math and science were concerned. It was as if he immediately knew he belonged by virtue of his abilities."

"So you're saying he should have stayed where he would be sheltered and never experience failure? While probably safer, where's the fun, the challenge?"

"I didn't mean it that way." She frowned. "Or maybe I did. Is it such a bad thing for me to want to protect my son from some of the harsh realities of life?"

"That depends."

She opened her mouth and he held up his hand. "Wait. Hear me out. When he was five, it was your job to protect him from harsh reality. Nurturing and teaching were two of your most important jobs. But that changes as our children approach adulthood. We have to stand there and watch, hearts in our throats, while they make mistakes and get hurt."

"Training for NASCAR is a little different than getting stood up for the prom."

"As they grow, the stakes get higher. Michael's an adult, ready to make mistakes of his own."

"That's what I'm afraid of."

"He'll have the security of knowing you love him, knowing he can talk things through with you. It's a gift."

"Wouldn't a fruit basket work just as well?" Her lips twitched.

He liked the way her brown eyes sparkled. "Are you laughing at me, Tess McIntyre?"

"No, laughing at myself. I'm well aware people consider me overprotective. Believe it or not, I'm really trying to allow Michael to make his own decisions, his own mistakes…"

"But nobody said it would be so damn hard," he completed for her. "Let me tell you a story about a father, his daughter and her boyfriend. It's a humiliating tale, but I bet it will make you feel much better."

"I can't wait to hear this." Tess popped a shrimp in her mouth.

"It was when my daughter, Stephanie, was nineteen—"

The door opened and several people entered. Sam recognized a few as executives of one of his sponsoring companies.

"I'm sorry, I need to go say hello. Excuse me?"

"Of course. But don't think you're getting out of telling me your humiliating tale."

"No, you wouldn't let me off the hook that easily." He stood, moving to greet his guests. Risking a glance over his shoulder, he was surprised to see Tess watching him carefully, her eyes dark and pensive. As if she was trying to figure him out. Or as if she…found him attractive.

The thought nearly made him trip over his own feet.

When he glanced her way again, her expression was carefully composed, as if she'd never had a remotely personal thought in her life. But he was beginning to know better.

MICHAEL STOOD behind the low wall, careful to stay out of the crew's way. His pulse pounded as the cars zoomed past. He watched closely as Sam's driver pulled into the pit and the crew jumped into action. It was choreographed chaos. And happened so fast, if he'd looked away, he might not have realized the car had even stopped.

Ron glanced up from the pit cart and gave him the thumbs-up before returning his attention to the computer monitor.

Michael couldn't help but grin. This was the big time. And he was right in the middle of it.

Once the drivers settled in and most of the cars were drafting, Michael relaxed. He eyed the sky, noting a few clouds, but no chance of rain. The wind was slight, maybe five miles per hour. He calculated the wind drag, taking into account track location, banking and surface, then adjusting for temperature. What would his strategy be if he were driving in this race?

Would he make a gutsy move, like trying to pass before the chicane, or series of turns? Risking that he could negotiate the quick right turn, left turn and right again?

He didn't know what he'd do and that was frustrating. Sam didn't seem to be in any hurry to put him in a car. The waiting was driving him nuts. He was so close, everything there for the taking, and he was stuck playing video games and working out in the gym.

A collective groan went up from the crowd. The spotter radioed about a wreck on the track. Then indicated their car was involved.

"Move it, kid." One of the crew jostled him out of the way as the crash cart was readied to make collision repairs. The driver was able to bring the car into the pits. Michael watched as sheets of colored tape were used to mold the damaged fender into a reasonable facsimile of its original aerodynamic form.

Michael calculated the change in wind drag and the effect it would have on the driver. If it were a restrictor-plate track, the guy might stand a chance. But, as it was, it looked as if he'd have a tough time getting maximum speed out of his car.

"You learning anything from all this?"

Michael's face warmed. He hadn't even heard Ron walk over. Michael felt as if he'd been given a pop quiz over material he hadn't studied. "Some."

"What'd our driver do wrong?"

"Got in a wreck?"

Ron shook his head, as if to say, "And this kid is a genius?"

"He was trying to make up speed in the chicane. Bad idea. Some drivers can pull it off, most can't."

"Yes, sir."

"Keep your eyes on the track and not on the sky, and you might pick up some pointers next time." Ron clapped him on the back to soften his words, but Michael still felt as if he'd been caught daydreaming during a test.

"But I—"

"I gotta get back, son. Keep your eyes peeled, okay?"

"Yes, sir."

"FOLKS, I'D LIKE you to meet Tess McIntyre." Sam drew the group of sponsors over to her.

Tess stood and shook hands all the way around.

"Tess is Michael McIntyre's mother. Michael is an exceptional talent we're bringing up."

"McIntyre," one gentleman said. "I don't recognize the name."

"You will," Sam said. "The kid's going to be the next young gun, you wait and see."

"You sure know talent." The man then eyed the buffet table, seemingly as intent on food as on discussing drivers.

"Please, help yourselves. We've got quite a spread of food and the bar's fully stocked. If you want something that's not there, we'll see that you have it next time."

The group murmured their thanks and descended on the buffet table.

Sam guided Tess to their seats. "The race is starting."

"How many cars do you have down there?"

"Two. I'd eventually like to build a team like the big ones, but it's a start."

"From what Michael says, it's an expensive sport."

"No doubt about it. Not like the old days when the drivers hauled their own cars in on a flatbed."

The voice of the announcer filled the room. Discussion tapered off as they waited for the green flag to drop.

Tess got caught up in the race. Glancing at Sam a few minutes later, he seemed totally absorbed.

"Which cars are yours?" she asked.

He told her and she smiled. His cars were running toward the front. Would Michael be down there someday? Did she want him to be down there someday?

Later, there was a minor on-track incident and the drivers pitted under a yellow flag.

Sam turned to her. "So what do you think?"

"I can certainly understand the appeal for an eighteen-year-old-boy running on testosterone and daring."

"But not for a guy approaching middle age like me?"

She covered her mouth with her hand. "I didn't mean it like that."

Sam smiled. "I'm just teasing you. Believe me, you're the epitome of tact. I imagine that makes you very good at what you do."

"I handle personal-injury cases. Tact is definitely an asset."

"And you're good at the injury stuff?"

"Yes, I am."

Her acknowledgment came as a surprise. "No 'Aw shucks, not really' deflection?"

She met his gaze. "There are too many times in life when I've had to admit I didn't have a clue. I've worked hard, learned as much as I possibly could. I've earned the right to say I'm good at what I do."

"If you're ever looking for a job, we might have something for you at Kincaid Racing. I've had times when I didn't have a clue, but I try to make sure that doesn't happen as much anymore. Although Michael threw me a curveball when he set up our first meeting."

"You and me both. How was one eighteen-year-old boy able to pull one over on us?"

Shaking his head, he said, "I'm still not sure. Scary, huh?"

"Terrifying." She chuckled.

Muted chatter from several conversations behind them melded to make a comfortable background noise.

"What do you think of Charlotte?" he asked.

"It's a lovely city. Very different from Phoenix, of course."

"How about the whole racing scene?"

She hesitated. "People are very dedicated to the sport—that's for sure."

"NASCAR fans are like no others. I saw my first race and I was hooked. Baseball, my obsession, dropped to a distant second."

Tess leaned back in her chair and eyed him. "So why'd you choose Michael?"

"Why not?" He was superstitious enough not to want to analyze his gut instinct.

"There have to be thousands of other guys just as talented as he is, with more experience."

"I can't explain it, Tess. It's a feeling I get when I watch him drive. When I talk to him and hear the amazing way his mind works."

Tess laughed. "I'm not sure I would have pushed him toward those gifted classes if I'd known he'd race."

"Yes, you would. Because he has a phenomenal talent and you wouldn't want him to waste it."

"We agree in that respect. I'm not sure we'll ever agree on which talent we're talking about. What if he's meant to discover a new law of physics or a cure for cancer? Can you really say it's worth it for him to become a driver?"

Sam raised an eyebrow. "Who's to say Michael can't do both? Race NASCAR and still find a cure for cancer?"

"I have to admit I never thought of it that way." She tucked her hair behind her ear. "You've given me something to consider."

"Darn, I was hoping you'd jump right over to my way of thinking."

She rolled her eyes. "I'm not a pushover."

"Sorry, forgot I was dealing with an expert in negotiation." He made a mental note not to forget it again. Tess would be a formidable ally or enemy, depending on how he handled her.

CHAPTER SIX

TESS THOUGHT Michael's smile would light up the whole city when she saw him in the pits after the race was over.

"Hey, Sam, that was really great." Michael's eyes flashed.

"Yep. Imagine what it would be like if we'd won."

"Your drivers caught a couple tough breaks, but came back in the end. Placing second and fourth after coming from the back is pretty impressive."

"But you think you could have done better." Sam's tone made it a statement rather than a question.

"Yes. I think I've got that series of quick turns figured out."

"Hello to you, too, Michael," Tess said.

"Oh, hi, Mom." Then he launched into his theories of how to beat the unusual aspects of the track.

Sam nodded, seeming to weigh Michael's suggestions. "What do you say we look into some regional races?"

Michael whooped. Seeing the absolute joy on his face, Tess nearly forgot her objections to his racing career. She had to admit, if only to herself, she'd never seen him this happy.

"Hey, Michael," one of the crew members called. "We're gonna go grab something to eat. Want to come?"

He glanced at Tess, eagerness evident in every line of his body. He wanted so terribly to belong, to be a part of this. If only he didn't seem so young and inexperienced compared to the rest of the crew. Then she might not worry so much. But she had to allow him to grow, to gain experience, even if it might be the hard way.

Swallowing hard, she said, "Go ahead. Do you have your hotel key?"

"Yes."

"Don't stay out too late."

"I won't." He jogged off to join the other guys.

Tess had the oddest feeling, as if he were slipping away.

"The hotel has a bar. Do you want to stop for a drink?" Sam asked.

"No, I think I'd just like to go to my room."

They returned to the hotel and said good-night in the lobby. Sam's room was two floors up.

Tess sighed with relief as she entered the hotel room. She changed into her pajamas and sat in the easy chair, clicking on the light. She soon immersed herself in the novel she'd started reading on the plane.

Soon, her eyes grew heavy and she had a hard time keeping them open. When her head nodded, she finally closed her book and angled herself in the chair so she could rest her cheek against the side.

Tess didn't want to admit she was waiting for Michael to come home. Her ears were tuned for noises in the next room, but it was quiet.

She awoke with a start, wondering where she was. Finally, her eyes focused on the hotel room and the bedside clock—2:00 a.m.

She stretched her arms over her head. A thump on the wall separating her room from Michael's startled her. She heard the muted sound of male voices. Then laughter.

Tess went to the connecting door and tapped lightly. "Michael?"

"I'm okay, Mom."

But something didn't sound quite right.

She flipped the lock and turned the knob. When she walked through, the aroma of beer and vomit hit her first.

The guy who'd invited Michael glanced everywhere but at Tess's face. "Sorry, ma'am. We didn't mean to wake you."

"You're getting in very late. Michael, we have a busy day ahead of us tomorrow. Today," she amended.

The other guy sensed it was time to get away. "See ya, Michael. It was good meeting you, Mrs. McIntyre."

"Tess. Goodbye."

Once the door shut behind him, Tess focused solely on Michael. He swayed on his feet, giving her a goofy half smile. His words were slurred when he said, "Had fun with the guys."

"That's obvious. Haven't we discussed the dangers of alcohol, especially in this kind of environment?"

He blinked but didn't answer.

"Michael, you reek of beer."

"Yeah, I had one of those."

"You're underage."

"The guys bought pitchers. It would have been rude to say no." He nodded, very satisfied with his explanation. "You always said...don't be rude."

She wanted to be angry at her son, but was too concerned about his health at the moment. Anger would come later. "You better get ready for bed before you pass out on your feet."

"That's a pretty good idea." The swaying intensified. His pallor took on a greenish tinge. "I don't feel s' good."

"I don't imagine you do."

"Gonna be—"

She propelled him toward the bathroom, flipped up the commode lid and stood back. "Sick." She completed the sentence for him, because he was occupied.

SAM KNEW something was wrong the minute he met Tess and Michael in the lobby the next morning.

Tess looked angry enough to spit nails. Michael looked as if he'd swallowed some and the meal wasn't sitting well.

"Morning, you two. I reserved a table for breakfast." Michael groaned.

"Thank you." Tess's voice was decidedly cool.

As they approached the café, Michael said, "I think I'm gonna skip breakfast," and hurried away.

"What's wrong with him? I have yet to see the kid pass up a meal."

"He's extremely hungover this morning."

"Ah." No wonder she was mad.

What had Michael been thinking? He was supposed to be proving to his mother that he was a mature adult. The problem being that Michael was like many eighteen-year-old boys—a man only in chronological age.

"How are you holding up?"

"I'm fine. Disappointed, but fine. This is just the reason I didn't want him traveling in a series without adequate supervision."

"Did you talk to him?"

"No, he's not receptive to much of anything right now, except an up-close-and-personal conversation with the porcelain gods."

Sam grinned. "That phrase takes me back."

"It's not funny." Tess rubbed her arms as if she were chilled. "To you, this might just be a harmless rite of passage. To me, it shows someone too immature to step up to the plate and handle his responsibilities."

The shadows in her eyes told him they weren't talking solely about Michael.

"You've had personal experience with this kind of thing?"

"I was never into the party scene in high school. And after that, I had a small child to take care of. My ex-husband was…conflicted about family life. He started spending more and more time out with the guys, came home pretty drunk…and just drifted away from us. Before I knew it, he'd taken a job out of the country. So, yes, the whole immature party stuff brings back memories of the beginning of the end."

Sam touched her arm, wanting to say something wise

to make her feel better. The best he could do was, "That sucks. No wonder it hits a chord."

She nodded, her eyes wide and begging for reassurance, though he was fairly sure she was unaware of her need.

"Hey, if Michael's as smart as I think he is, he'll learn from this experience. Especially if you and I counsel him a bit."

"You'd do that?" Her voice was husky.

"Absolutely. How about if I go talk to him right now? I might be able to find out what happened last night before he goes into full defensive mode."

"Thanks, Sam. That might be the best way to handle it. I'll wait here till our table's called."

Sam crossed the lobby and went out the double doors. He glanced around, spying Michael sitting on a bench under a shade tree, his head cradled in his hands.

No doubt about it, the kid was hurting. And Sam also had no doubt it was time for some tough love. For worrying his mother at the very least.

"You want to tell me what happened last night?" He used his father-of-the-juvenile-delinquent voice.

Michael raised his head and groaned, shielding his eyes from the sunlight. "I had a few beers with the guys."

"Looks like you had more than a few."

"I lost count."

"You do realize that was the absolute stupidest thing you could have done, don't you?"

"Everyone does it."

Sam so didn't want to be having this conversation. He'd heaved a great sight of relief when both his kids had graduated college, figuring these types of situations were in the past. He told himself he'd do it to protect his investment in Michael. But he had a niggling suspicion he'd do it as much for Tess as for himself.

"Is everyone else this close—" he pinched his thumb and forefinger together "—to getting their dream ride? A shot at NASCAR?"

"I dunno."

"You know, for a genius, you sound pretty dumb right now. That's what alcohol does."

Defiance flashed in Michael's eyes. "You don't own me, dude. My mom treats me like a kid. I'm eighteen, an adult."

"And you think drinking till you puke is mature? Breaking the law is a good thing? If you do, I seriously overestimated your character."

"Hey, back off. You're not my dad."

Michael's attitude had Sam seeing red. He stepped forward, crowding the kid. "No, I'm not. I'm the man who signs your paychecks. Who says whether you'll have a space on my team. I'm the one who told your mother how much you'd matured and that you were ready to go on the road and get some regional races under your belt. And then you go and do this. You say you want to be treated like an adult. Then how about acting like one at least long enough for your mother to be reassured and head on back to Phoenix?"

Michael groaned. "Oh, man, she'll never let me out of her sight now."

"This just occurred to you? And by the way, my name isn't man or dude. I expect you to address me by

Sam or Mr. Kincaid. *If* I decide to keep you on my team, you'll be dealing with members of the press. I'll want you to come across as intelligent, grounded and respectful. If you don't think you can achieve that, let me know right now and you and your mama can fly back to Phoenix today. If you decide to stay, grow up. I'm not your mama and I don't intend to put up with any BS. I won't wipe your nose and I won't kiss your boo-boos to make them better. Got it?"

Michael straightened. "Yes, sir. I just wanted to be a regular guy for once."

"Well, you're not a regular guy," Sam barked. "Get used to it and be glad you've been given an opportunity that most only dream of."

"Yes, Sam."

"Now, get in there and apologize to your mother for worrying her. Then eat a good breakfast. Your stomach isn't going to feel better till you get food."

"I can't eat."

"You can and will. Now get."

Sam stood under the tree for a few minutes after Michael left, trying to regain some composure. The drill-sergeant role didn't come naturally, but darn if it didn't seem necessary with a kid like Michael McIntyre.

For the first time, he found himself wondering what in the heck he'd been thinking to hire an eighteen-year-old boy chafing at his mama's apron strings.

TESS WATCHED Michael's color return after he ate a few pancakes. His appetite seemed to return, too, and he shoveled pancakes in his mouth at an alarming rate.

Michael chewed, swallowed and took a long drink of milk. "So when do I get to do some real racing?"

"You need to be solid on the sim before we put you on the track. I want the good driving habits to be so ingrained, you'll be less likely to pick up bad habits. And believe me, there are plenty out there."

"I *do* have the good habits ingrained. I'm not an idiot for gosh's sake. I beat the simulator almost every time."

"Almost isn't good enough."

For once, Tess agreed wholeheartedly. Where Michael's safety was concerned, only one hundred percent would be good enough in her book.

Michael sighed heavily. "I'm so bored I can't see straight. Maybe I should have gone to Stanford." He eyed Sam expectantly.

Tess could barely believe this was her son. First the drinking, now this new, underhanded approach. When had her son become manipulative? A dose of his own medicine would do him good.

She rose. "Since that's decided, we better get back to Charlotte. We'll want to pack and be ready to leave first thing in the morning. We still have time to sign you up for classes."

"But—" Michael and Sam said in unison.

She raised her hand to stop them. "You heard Michael, Sam. He's made up his mind. Nothing you or I say will dissuade him."

Sam held her gaze for a moment. Then leaned back in the booth, as if waiting to see how this played out.

"Man, Mom, don't take me so literally."

"How did you intend for me to take you?"

He shifted in his seat. "It wasn't meant for you. I was talking to Sam."

"And what was your goal in making this statement?"

"I'm a grown man and you're making way too big a deal out of this."

"Am I? I don't think so. You didn't like it just now when I manipulated you. Was your blatant attempt at manipulation with Sam any better?"

"So it was the blatant part you objected to? Next time I'll try to be more subtle." His tone was sullen.

"Mr. Kincaid has invested a lot of time in training you. He could potentially invest a lot of money, too. He deserves you to act like a man and treat him honestly."

"How can I act like a man when I have my mommy tagging along everywhere I go?"

Tess inhaled sharply. She'd always been grateful that Michael had seemed to escape the typical teenage attitude. Apparently, she'd been too hasty.

"Michael," Sam said, his tone stern, "your mother is absolutely right. If you have a beef with the way I'm handling your training, you need to be up-front and discuss it with me. Your mother also deserves to be treated with respect."

Tess shook her head in wonder. So this was what it would have been like if Michael'd had a father who took an active role. It was unsettling, but on the whole…reassuring. For once, she felt as if she could take a breath and relax her guard because someone had her back.

"I'm sorry." Michael's tone was sincere. "I'm just frustrated with all the waiting."

"Apology accepted," she said.

"So if I ace the sim, how long will it be before I can hit some of the regional races?"

"You just ace the sim and then we'll talk."

"Okay." His voice was glum, but he managed to finish off his tall stack of pancakes.

MICHAEL LOVED the power as he accelerated. Nothing had prepared him for the feel of all those horses beneath the hood of the expensive machine.

He accelerated around the track, experimenting with his shifting, keeping his line low on the track. Then he experimented high. Sam waved him in all too soon.

Michael pulled into the pit area, overshooting by a good ten feet. Damn. He'd have to practice his pit stops. Then again, even the guys running in NASCAR NEXTEL Cup Series still regularly practiced pit stops, or so he'd been told.

Sam walked over. "You ready for some competition?"

"Sure."

Several stock cars pulled out of the garage area and onto the track.

"These are some of my friends. I called in a few favors and they're gonna run with you."

"Sweet."

"We'll have you start at pole the first time, see how you do with that. Next time it'll be from the back."

The adrenaline rush of racing gave him courage. "Believe me, I won't be starting from the back by the time I get to Busch."

"Those are some big words you might have to eat."

Michael shook his head. "I've got to set the bar high. If my expectations are mediocre, chances are my performance will match."

"One of your teachers tell you that?"

"Nah, just the opposite. They thought I needed to chill out more. I made them nervous."

"I bet you did." Sam rapped on the hood. "Now, go line up. These guys don't have all day."

Michael pulled the car into pole position. The blue car started next to him, the driver giving him a thumbs-up. Michael returned the gesture, wondering who might be behind the blue full-face helmet. The number was taped over, as if the guy wanted to remain anonymous.

A red car lined up behind him and a yellow car next to him.

Sam held the flag.

Michael's muscles tensed as he tried to remember how to start well from the pole position. He panicked when his mind went blank.

Sam brought the green flag down.

Instinct kicked in and Michael accelerated, running smoothly through the gears.

The blue car tried to take the lead, but Michael held it off. They battled, nose to nose, with the other two cars breathing down his neck.

Find your line.

He concentrated hard, but finally had to give in to instinct. All his hard-learned lessons had disappeared.

At lap nine, Sam waved the white flag, signifying there was one more lap.

Then the battle with the blue car happened in earnest.

Michael was able to hold it off for another half lap. Then the driver went high, accelerated in a burst of speed and passed him. The driver of the blue car won the checkered flag.

Michael swallowed disappointment.

The simulators had been easy in comparison. Real competition with pro drivers brought a whole new dimension into play.

He followed the blue car, exiting the track to the garage stalls. Michael pulled into the stall next to the blue car.

The driver maneuvered himself out the window and removed his helmet.

Michael's mouth dropped open.

Mark LeBeau, his idol.

He'd run neck and neck with Mark LeBeau—who'd have thought?

Certainly not his friends, who'd accused him of making up stories about driving NASCAR to begin with. Certainly not his mom, who felt he should never have a thought that wasn't strictly academic. And not his dad, who was rarely in the States, and when he was, didn't seem to be in a hurry to spend time with his only son.

Mark came over and extended his hand. "Not bad, kid."

"Thank you, sir. It's an honor."

"No, the honor's mine. I have the feeling we're gonna see a lot more of you out there."

"I sure hope so."

Sam and his mother walked up. His mother smiled, but he could tell she was worried all the same.

He introduced her to Mark, his tone slightly awed. Just when he wanted to sound cool and collected.

"Sam, the kid's everything you said and more."

Sam nodded. "Thanks, Mark. Appreciate it."

"We're even now, aren't we?"

"You bet."

When Mark left, Sam eyed Michael. "What'd you think?"

"It wasn't what I expected. But you were right about all that simulator stuff—most of the moves became automatic."

"You held your own, kid, with a more than worthy opponent. Try to imagine being out there with forty-two Marks, at the top of their games."

Michael did try to imagine it. Swallowing hard, he realized for the first time exactly what he was up against. Being good wasn't enough. He had to be phenomenal.

"I think I've got a lot of work to do."

Sam nodded. "I was hoping you'd say that. It means you're ready to tackle the next step. What do you say about setting up some regional races?"

"Let's do it." The fire in his gut hadn't abated. But it was tempered with a healthy dose of reality. No doubt about it, he needed to grow up, get over himself and get down to business.

Michael wondered if that was what being a man was all about.

CHAPTER SEVEN

TESS WANDERED through the condo, shifting a picture, squaring the coffee table, almost wishing Charlotte were in the middle of a dust bowl. At least then she could dust every day and feel useful.

Michael was working with his trainer, learning the ins and outs of driving on dirt tracks.

With five more months of this, Tess would go bonkers if she didn't find something constructive to do. And here she'd always thought early retirement sounded like a good idea. Ha! Sure, the ability to sleep late and not be tied to a schedule had appealed the first couple weeks. But now she felt as if she needed to find her own identity in Charlotte. More than simply a hanger-on to her son.

Tess shuddered at the thought. She'd always worked hard and earned the respect of her superiors and co-workers. Being merely competent had never been enough.

She rescued her abandoned needlepoint project tossed on the couch. Putting it away in the project bag, she had a sneaking suspicion she would be grateful to be too busy for needlework.

Nodding her head, she came to a decision. She grabbed her purse and keys and headed out the door.

Twenty minutes later, Tess smoothed her hair as she crossed the parking lot to the offices of Kincaid Racing. The two-story building of red brick and glass gave the impression of being both established and contemporary at the same time.

When she walked in, the reception area was large, with a soaring ceiling. A huge Oriental rug defined the seating area, covering hardwood floors.

She introduced herself to the receptionist, a woman with steel-gray hair and an aura that was part drill instructor, part mother hen.

"I'm here to see Sam Kincaid."

"Do you have an appointment?"

"No, but I was hoping he might have a spare moment. I'm Michael McIntyre's mother."

Recognition flashed in the woman's eyes. "I've met Michael a few times. He's got a good head on his shoulders."

"I'm glad to hear that—" Tess glanced at the woman's nameplate "—Shirley."

Shirley grinned. "Please have a seat and I'll let Sam know you're here."

A few minutes later, Sam came out to greet her. Smiling, he said, "Tess, this is a terrific surprise. Come on back."

"I hope I'm not interrupting anything important. It was a spur-of-the-moment decision."

"You and Michael are two of my top priorities."

And he meant it. It was oddly reassuring to know he

didn't seem to mind dropping everything for her. Royce, her ex, had been pretty unwilling to rearrange anything in his life to make room for his wife and son. That trend had continued after the divorce and throughout Michael's childhood.

Glancing around, Tess was impressed. Sam's office was huge. It shouldn't surprise her really. As team owner, it stood to reason he would have the very best. Sometimes she forgot he was a successful entrepreneur and racing big shot. Maybe because of his down-to-earth attitude.

"Have a seat." He directed her to a grouping of leather easy chairs and a love seat. "Would you like coffee or a soft drink?"

"No, thank you. I won't stay long. I just wanted to run an idea past you."

"Sure." He sat in the chair next to her. She was glad they didn't have the huge expanse of cherry-wood desk between them. The ornate desk was on a riser in front of the bank of floor-to-ceiling windows. The view was breathtaking, a dense, deep-green forest. "What's your idea?"

"I'm finding I'm at loose ends now that more of Michael's training is on the track."

"I don't think it would be a good idea for you to spend more time at the track. I'd like Michael to devote all his attention to the job at hand."

Tess raised an eyebrow. "You mean it's good for him to have time away from his hovering mother?"

"You don't hover, Tess. But, yes, it's good for him to stand on his own two feet."

"I'd like to get an idea what our travel schedule will look like in the coming months. I'll go stir-crazy if I sit around the condo the whole time we're in town. I intend to find a part-time job or volunteer opportunity. But I need to know when I'll be available."

Sam leaned back in his chair. "We'll be traveling nearly every weekend. Flying or driving on Thursday. Racing Friday and Saturday nights. Home on Sunday. But it's not absolutely necessary for you to be there."

"Yes, it is. The drinking episode while we were at Seneca Lake only proves Michael needs guidance."

"Okay." Sam shrugged. "But he gets into trouble, he's all yours."

"Thanks, I appreciate that." Her tone was wry. "I'll still have Monday, Tuesday and Wednesday. It might be difficult to find an employer to accommodate those days. Volunteer work might be more flexible. Do you know any charities in need of a volunteer?"

"Hmm. Let me think for a minute." He gazed out the window. "I spend some time at the food bank. Then there's a literacy program that many of the drivers' wives sponsor. I think Shirley volunteers there, too."

Sam mentioned his own volunteer work in such an offhanded way, her respect for him grew. He didn't grandstand.

Tess smiled. "I love books. I love teaching. Literacy sounds perfect."

"Good, I'll have Shirley copy the information for you. Say, have it ready when we return from lunch?"

Tess's face warmed. "I didn't come here angling for a lunch invitation."

"I didn't think you did. I'd like you to join me. Is there anything wrong with that?"

"Not at all." In fact, his suggestion made her smile in anticipation. Since when had she started looking forward to spending time with Sam?

SAM CHOSE his favorite little Italian place. He didn't stop to analyze why he felt comfortable taking Tess there, when he rarely brought the women he dated.

It was a restaurant without pretense, just excellent food and a warm, family-like atmosphere. He pulled out the chair for Tess, wondering if it was a lame, old-fashioned gesture.

Her wide smile told him it was okay.

The owner's son, Giovanni, greeted him. "Ah, Signor Kincaid, it is so good to see you again."

"Thank you, Giovanni."

"Signora." He placed the napkin on Tess's lap.

"Grazi, Signore."

"You speak Italian?"

"Only a little."

"Bene."

He handed them menus and murmured a promise to return for their orders.

"Everything looks wonderful," Tess said. "Smells wonderful, too."

"The chef will prepare to order, if there's something you'd like that isn't on the menu."

"During lunch? Boy, you must be very special."

"No, they treat everyone the same. That's one of the reasons I like this place."

"I can see why."

"How did you learn Italian?"

"I listened to an audio course in the car during my commute. I picked up just enough to be dangerous."

"You do better than I do."

She glanced down at her menu, her lashes shadowing her skin. "Thank you."

"Why Italian? Aren't there more Spanish-speaking folks in Arizona?"

"Yes, and I learned a bit of Spanish by audio, too. I've always wanted to travel to Italy. Learning a bit of Italian was kind of like promising myself I'd someday speak the language in Rome, Venice, Tuscany. All those wonderful, warm places."

This side of Tess intrigued him. Maybe there was a bit of a dreamer in her soul, after all.

"Phoenix isn't warm enough for you?" he asked.

"Plenty. I meant the warm atmosphere, the people."

"I think I understand. Probably the same reason I come here when I want to enjoy a good meal without having to deal with pretensions."

Tess laughed, her brown eyes alight with amusement. "I'm flattered you brought me. I guess that means you don't find me pretentious."

"No, definitely not pretentious. More like careful. Besides, I can't think of anyone I'd rather have lunch with."

She tilted her head. "What a nice thing to say."

"It's the truth." He reached across the table and squeezed her hand.

She returned the pressure, then withdrew her hand

on the pretext of reaching for her water glass. "What about you? Do you have a list of things you want to do before you die?"

"I'm doing it. Kincaid Racing is my dream, my ultimate challenge. I love the thrill of pulling together a team, finding the most talented drivers and putting them in optimum equipment."

"And what about after that? Any other dreams?"

He paused to mull over her question, unexpected and slightly unsettling. "Most people are impressed with my business success and the fact that I've bought a NASCAR team, all before fifty. You keep me humble."

"I didn't mean to offend you. I just thought a man as intelligent as you with such a zest for life must have a zillion things you want to do. You're the kind of man I imagine moving from one challenge to the next, never completely satisfied with status quo."

"Status quo is highly overrated."

"But safe," she murmured.

"Not always. But I won't argue the point. Are you ready to order?"

"What do you recommend?"

"The veal is excellent. I like the tortellini, chicken Parmesan. Everything's good."

The waiter came by and Tess consulted with him in halting Italian before choosing an eggplant dish.

Sam ordered the veal by rote. He was busy trying to figure out Tess. She'd asked for his recommendations, then ignored them.

She was definitely her own woman. And he liked that.

She leaned forward, interrupting his train of thought.

"Michael's very excited to start the regional races. He thinks he can leap tall buildings with a single bound now that he's held his own on the track with Mark LeBeau."

"A little bit of confidence is a good thing."

"As long as he stays grounded. Before racing came into our lives, I wouldn't have worried. But now, I'm afraid it could go to his head."

"Michael's working hard. With the exception of the drinking episode in Seneca Lake, I've noticed a new maturity in his approach to things. And there's a learning curve involved. But if I think he's getting too full of himself, I'll rein him in. If not, the ups and downs of racing will put him in a more realistic frame of mind."

She tilted her head. "You almost sound like you want him to fail."

"Yes, within reason. I want to see how he picks himself up and works through it. Drivers have to be tenacious, because the hard times come to everyone, no matter how gifted."

The waiter delivered their food.

"This looks wonderful." Tess smiled, but her eyes were shadowed.

"What's wrong?"

"Nothing. You've just given me something to think about."

"Now that scares me. Did I say something to worry you?"

"I'm starting to see things differently here in Charlotte. Maybe I made a mistake protecting Michael from failure. I'm afraid he won't know how to bounce back."

"None of us want to see our children fail. But it's a

part of life. If he doesn't learn now, it may come back to bite him on the rear later."

"When he's around, Michael's father encourages him to take risks. It drives me crazy because the two of them are having a great time and I'm the one worrying over the what-ifs."

"I take it his father's not around much?"

"Royce drops in from time to time. Shows Michael the world, does his superdad thing, then leaves again."

"His loss."

"Yes. But Michael deserved a dad who was there for him one hundred percent, not an overgrown teen chasing the next adrenaline rush."

Sam wondered about Tess's relationship with her ex-husband. How had two apparently totally opposite people fallen in love in the first place? And why was she hanging on to resentments from a marriage that had ended so long ago? He told himself it didn't matter. All that mattered was Michael and his ability to race.

Yeah, right.

CHAPTER EIGHT

IT WAS Saturday night in Greenville, South Carolina, and Tess didn't think she'd been more nervous in her life.

"Good luck, sweetheart." She gave Michael a kiss.

"Aw, Mom."

"Sorry, I forgot, no public displays of affection from Mom. I'll go find a seat in the stands before I do anything else embarrassing."

"Save me a seat," Sam called, smiling in reassurance, as if he understood how hard it was for her to pry herself away from her son before his first regional race.

But when he joined her in the stands, Sam seemed to have a hard time sitting still.

"I'm not the only one with prerace jitters," she observed.

"I don't know why it's harder this time. We've seen him race against other drivers before."

"But that was for fun. Before extensive training. You're probably wondering the same thing I am. What if the training actually did more harm than good?"

He glanced sideways at her. "Yeah, but I'll deny it to anyone else. I hope we didn't mess up that raw spark he had."

Tess grasped his hand and squeezed. "Relax, it'll be fine."

It felt odd to reassure Sam after all the times he'd reassured her. Odd, but somehow right. Especially when he squeezed her hand in return.

"You're a fraud, Sam Kincaid."

"Say what?"

"You had me believing you knew exactly what you were doing designing a regimen for Michael. But training a driver isn't an exact science like you led me to believe."

He grinned. "You found me out. What works for one driver could be the absolute worst approach for another. That's one of the things that makes recruiting and training drivers so exciting. It also makes it risky."

"I'll pretend you didn't say that. *Risk* is a four-letter word in my book."

Laughing, Sam said, "I never would have guessed. But *luck* is a four-letter word, too, and right now we've got it on our side. I'm glad we found a ready-made regional crew when one of the teams went bankrupt."

Tess nudged him with her shoulder. "Gosh, good thing they went bankrupt."

"That's not how I meant it."

"I know. I couldn't resist teasing you. I may not ever get another opportunity to see you this vulnerable. You're normally so darn self-assured."

"I'm *not* vulnerable. But being terrified can be a good thing. It lets me know I'm taking risks. Sorry, I used that word again."

"So long as you don't take those risks with my son's safety."

He held her gaze. "I would never do that. Never."

She'd made the comment partially in jest, but his response reassured her in a way she hadn't expected.

"You're a good man, Sam."

"We'll see if you say that when the probationary period is up."

Tess had the feeling she'd gotten too close to the truth. Or he was uncomfortable with praise.

She glanced sideways, studying him without being too obvious. He hadn't dropped her hand, hadn't scooted down the bleacher to put more space between them. But he couldn't seem to take his gaze from the infield now that they were gearing up for the race.

He *was* a good man.

And he deserved to be down on the infield where the action was. "You know, with a new team and such, I'd feel better if you were down there keeping an eye on things."

"No, I'll stay up here with you." His voice held a trace of resignation.

"No, I insist. And I'm sure it would be better for Michael to have someone familiar down there."

"Are you sure?"

"Positive." She smiled.

"Come find us when the race is over?"

"I promise."

He stood, then began taking the steps two at a time.

TESS CHEERED HERSELF nearly hoarse as Michael crossed the finish line in first place and captured the checkered flag.

She was eager to see her son, but it took precious time to wend her way through the crowd. Finally, she made it to the pit area where she found him. She gave him a big hug. "You did it, sweetheart."

Michael grinned from ear to ear, seemingly unaware that she'd already broken his policy against PDAs.

"It was great, Mom. So much better this time since I've come across most of the situations in the simulators."

"I'm glad. I was cheering like crazy for you."

He cleared his throat. "Were you really?"

"Of course. I'm your mother."

"Even if you don't totally approve?"

"I'm always in your corner. Don't ever doubt that."

Sam came over and touched her arm to get her attention. "What did you think?"

Tess couldn't help but smile in triumph. "I think he looked like a champion."

"I did, too."

TESS HUMMED as she set out festive fall decorations she'd found at a craft fair. She intended to scour discount and thrift stores for Halloween decorations—Halloween had always been one of Michael's favorite holidays.

It was the first weekend they'd been in town for over a month. Michael had won first place at regional tracks every weekend and continued to leave the competition in the dust.

Slowly, Tess had begun to accept that Sam might have been right. It appeared her son had a special gift where driving stock cars was concerned. NASCAR was the pinnacle and Stanford was becoming more and more a might-have-been.

The realization made her sad, but not as sad as it once might have. She was starting to accept that he was becoming a man who had the right to choose his own path. Ill-advised though it might turn out to be.

There was also something freeing in the realization. Because it meant she'd done a good job raising her son. Good enough that he had the confidence to try new things. She might not have understood that had Sam not pointed it out.

Tess smiled. Her truce with Sam was an unexpected bonus that was turning into friendship. Maybe change wasn't such a bad thing.

Michael came out of his room, dressed and alert, not an early-Saturday-morning norm for him. At least not until Charlotte.

Her heart sank. He looked too purposeful, not like a guy preparing to spend the morning lounging on the couch, remote in hand. Or spending a few precious hours with his mother.

"Good morning. Pancakes or waffles?"

"I gotta run, Mom. I'll catch something on the way to the track. I'm meeting Ron so he can give me some pointers, then heading to the gym."

"I thought maybe we could spend some time together…."

"I'd love to, but no time." He grabbed an apple from the fruit bowl on the counter, kissed her on the cheek and headed out the door.

She stood in the middle of the great room clutching an assortment of minipumpkins, her optimism waning. Where the heck had her life gone? It seemed that just yesterday Michael had started kindergarten, lost his first tooth, had his first crush. And now he was gone.

Tess blinked back tears. The idea of Michael becoming an adult was no longer abstract. Nor was the concept of an empty nest. The accompanying pang of loss was very real. So real, it brought back how alone she'd felt after Michael's father left—the almost physical ache of being left behind.

Tess took a deep breath to will away the panicky impulse to run after Michael and hold on tightly so he couldn't leave. She hated the pathetic creature she'd turned into at the thought of being alone. She was strong; she had interests of her own. And she would get through it when Michael eventually left home.

The phone rang. Tess picked up the handset, grateful for a reprieve from the silence.

It was Sam. Her pulse jumped, but then she realized he probably called for Michael.

"Hi, Sam, you just missed him. Michael already left."

"You're the one I wanted to talk to."

"Oh."

"Do you have plans this afternoon?"

Other than feeling sorry for myself?

"No, I'd intended to spend some time with Michael, but he left in a whirlwind of activity." There, she'd managed to keep the whine out of her voice.

"Yeah, he's got a pretty full schedule. I thought

maybe you'd be up for a drive, see a little of the countryside. There's an arts-and-crafts festival I thought you might enjoy."

Tess resisted the urge to thank him profusely and promise to wait on the curb till he arrived. Instead, she went for a more nonchalant response. "I suppose—"

"There are a few antique stores on the way, from what I understand," he prodded, not that he needed to bother.

Laughing, she said, "I certainly can't say no to antiquing. Are you sure you're up to it?"

"Positive."

"In that case, I'd love to."

"Can you be ready in an hour? We can stop for lunch. Make it a day?"

"Sounds like a plan."

"Great. See you in an hour."

Tess hung up the phone, smiling at her own eagerness. Was it simply relief at having a reprieve from the whole empty-nest contemplation, or because she was looking forward to spending the day with Sam?

Shrugging, she decided it didn't matter. Suddenly, her day looked promising again.

SAM GLANCED at Tess in the passenger seat and grinned. "I'm glad you were able to make it. Kept me from rattling around the house or hanging over Ron's shoulder while he works with Michael."

"Believe me, I'm the one who was rescued." Her eyes narrowed. "But then again, I suspect you know that."

Shrugging, he said, "You're a long way from home and I haven't left you much time to look into volunteering. I just thought you might be at loose ends. If you were in Phoenix, you'd probably welcome some time to yourself or to hang out with your friends."

"Yes…with my friends." There were a few women from work she lunched with, but by and large, her life revolved around Michael and making a home for him. She was starting to realize how isolated her life had become.

Soon, Tess lost herself in the view of the countryside. "I love all the greenery and the huge trees. We don't have much of that in Phoenix."

"But you've got all that great cactus and desert."

"I've lived there most of my life, so I guess it's hard to appreciate what's always been there."

"I suppose so. I look at all the green and see humidity and chiggers."

Tess chuckled. "True."

"How do you think Michael's doing?" he asked.

"He seems to really respect Ron."

"I think they'll be a good team. I'm glad I was able to free up Ron to spend some time with him."

"So it was intentional? I thought maybe Ron simply had some extra time to kill."

Sam glanced at her, raising an eyebrow, then returned his attention to the road. "During the season? No way. He's a top crew chief in high demand. I've got another chief working with him, getting a feel for how he works with my other driver. Then, if everything works out, I'd like to team Ron with Michael next February."

"For the Busch Series?"

"Yes. It's a huge step, but I think Michael will be up to the challenge. I'm almost afraid to ask what you think."

Tess hesitated. "I don't have that knee-jerk reaction anymore, where I was positive that there's only one best course for Michael."

"I appreciate how hard you've tried to keep an open mind. I know it hasn't been easy."

"No, it hasn't. And there's still a long way to go."

"And a short time to get there. Up ahead is one of those antique stores I found online. You want to stop?"

"Of course."

After Sam parked the car, they walked into the shop. It was crowded with an assortment of old knickknacks and furniture. He was starting to get accustomed to the crowded chaos after a lifetime of open, airy stores where he pointed to the furniture he liked, selected a color and made arrangements to have it delivered.

The rapt expression on Tess's face as she examined a vase told him she'd take this store any day over the chain variety, high end or not.

"Is this what you'd call a treasure hunt?" he asked.

"You remembered?"

"Sure. Our first antiquing session."

"Yes, this is a treasure hunt." Her eyes sparkled. "You never know what you're going to find."

"I guess not." Her enthusiasm was catching. Wandering through the store, Sam intended to find some treasures of his own. He picked up an old tin that had been tucked away in a corner. It contained an assortment of old fishing lures. Hand-carved and painted, one of a kind, he was sure.

"Those are beautiful," she said. "Great for a shadow box arrangement."

He glanced sideways at her. "I was thinking of using them to catch fish."

She smiled. "Or there's that."

"You're not appalled that I'd risk damaging them?"

"That's their intended use. You should get as much enjoyment out of them as possible. They're only things."

"Hmm. Interesting viewpoint. You enjoy beautiful things, you take care of them, but you don't get bent out of shape if other people don't."

"Relationships and people are what count, not things. I try not to get bent out of shape by the unimportant stuff."

"Which relationships do you value most?" The question bordered on touchy-feely, but he was curious.

"My son, of course. My parents, who live in New Mexico now. A few friends…"

"Boyfriends?" He'd stepped over a line, but couldn't seem to stop himself.

Tess glanced away, pretending to be fascinated with a vintage Dr. Seuss book. "I used to read this to Michael all the time."

She placed the book on the shelf and turned to him. "No, my lifestyle hasn't been conducive to boyfriends. I'd thought early on Michael should have a father figure, but it didn't work out."

An older gentleman came from the back room. "Afternoon, folks. You see anything you're interested in, give me a holler."

They agreed and he returned to the back room.

"You said a father figure for Michael. What about a relationship for you?"

Her eyes narrowed. "I'm willing to answer that as long as you agree to be on the hot seat next. Are you sure you want me to do that?"

He laughed. "I was out of line. Sorry. I have to admit, I'm trying to figure you out."

Shrugging, she said, "What's to figure? I have a fulfilling career and a wonderful son."

"And that's enough?"

"Yes." But she wouldn't look him in the eye. "Now, let's see if we can find something for you to start collecting if you intend to use the lures. What are your interests besides racing and fishing?"

He thought about it for a minute. "I read, I bowl, I golf occasionally. I used to play baseball when I was younger. And, of course, there's the boating that goes along with the fishing."

Tess tilted her head. "I wouldn't have pegged you for a bowler."

"Yep, since I was a teen. Just to unwind, get life in perspective. Now you know my deep, dark secret. I hope that hasn't forever changed your impression of me."

She laughed. "It certainly makes you seem more… human."

"I guess I can accept that. I was afraid you might have detected my inner nerd."

"Not hardly." Moving through the maze of furniture, she stopped to look more closely at an old photo in a silver frame. "And bowling helps you get life in perspective?"

"A few hours on the lanes and I'm a new man. Nothing like wearing shoes hundreds of other feet have worn to keep a man humble."

She wrinkled her nose. "Now that you put it that way…"

"What do you do to get perspective?"

"What we're doing right now. Imagining the history of some of these pieces, the families who've used them. It tends to bring out the bigger picture to me."

"I guess I can see that. Though I think bowling is far superior. Since you've introduced me to your way of de-stressing, I'll have to take you bowling sometime."

Tess glanced up, frowning slightly. "You don't have to feel obligated to entertain me."

Yes, he did. For some reason, Sam felt compelled to make things right for her.

"Did you ever stop to think I might enjoy your company?"

"No…yes…I don't know."

How did such an intelligent, pretty woman come to be so clueless?

"Well, I do. Now, didn't you say you were going to figure out something for me to collect?"

"You collect race cars," she pointed out. "I've seen how many of them you have in the shop."

"Yeah, well, that's not collecting. It's just having the right equipment on hand."

"Sure, it is. I guess we can look for some vintage

bowling paraphernalia, though that might be hard to come by."

"I collected baseball cards as a kid."

Her eyes lit. "Ah, now we're getting somewhere. Baseball cards are highly collectible. Do you still have them?"

"No. My dad sold them at a yard sale after I moved out."

"What a shame. Maybe you can build a bigger, better collection." She moved to the counter and called out, "Sir?"

The owner came out of the front room. "Yes?"

"Do you have any baseball cards?"

"No, Wayne at the Collector's Emporium snags them as soon as I get them in. Marks them up excessively in my opinion."

"It was worth a try."

"Anything else I can help you with?"

"No, thank you."

He turned, then stopped. "Wait a minute, I did get an autographed ball in the other day. Signed by some of the Cubs players."

Sam could hardly believe his ears. It was all he could do not to jump over the counter and tell the guy he'd take it, right here, right now, name his price.

"I might be interested."

The old guy went to an old buffet table, where the ball was displayed almost as an afterthought.

He brought the clear plastic case over and handed it to Sam.

Sam held his breath as he gingerly picked up the ball

with his thumb and forefinger. Squinting, he was able to make out a few of the autographs. Cubs team of '85. The year he figured he would have been in the majors. Four years of college, one year in the minors, then the starting lineup for the Chicago Cubs.

Sam tried to keep his expression neutral, but Tess must have seen a spark of excitement.

She said, "It's really not what we're looking for...but I hate Sam to go home empty-handed." Then she negotiated like crazy and purchased the ball for a very reasonable price.

"Here, let me pay for it."

"No, it's a gift." Her voice was firm, no-nonsense. He had the feeling it was her paralegal voice.

"Thank you."

"You're very welcome. But before you think my reasons are completely altruistic, just know that I consider this bait. I'm looking for an antiquing buddy and if I'm not mistaken, you're hooked."

"I wouldn't count on it."

She smiled knowingly. "We'll see."

He doubted he'd spend afternoons scouring flea markets and antique stores on a regular basis. It was a way to pass time with Tess, a means to an end.

All the same, he found himself anticipating what other sports memorabilia they might find at the next stop....

TESS REACHED her condo door and hesitated. "I had such a good time, Sam. And thank you for walking me to the door."

"I had a pretty good time myself. Although I didn't

do as good a job haggling for the baseball cards as you did negotiating the ball. You'd think I'd never brokered a deal in my life."

Tess laughed, the sound washing over him in waves. She had a beautiful laugh. "You wanted it too badly. Once they know that, you're pretty much toast."

"No kidding. But I still think it was a productive day. Thanks again for the ball."

"My pleasure." Her words were almost formal, but the warmth of her tone sent awareness thrumming through him.

It was dark, the glow of the hall light illuminating her face. Tess had smooth skin and soft, silky hair. She seemed so much more than Michael's mom.

He brushed a strand away from her cheek. Leaning closer, he bent to brush his lips against the corner of her mouth. Not a seductive kiss, but not totally platonic, either. A testing kiss.

She didn't haul off and slug him. Her eyes widened, and she drew in a breath.

What would she do if he kissed her in earnest?

The door opened and Michael stood silhouetted. "Where have you been, Mom? I've been worried. I called your cell phone and got no answer."

"I'm sorry, Michael, my battery must've died."

Michael grinned, but there was an edge to his voice when he said, "Yeah, like I haven't used that one before."

"I took your mother to an arts-and-crafts fair. We knew you'd be busy all day training with Ron, so it didn't occur to us to check in."

Was this a role reversal or what?

"Was it your idea or Ron's to have Mom stay away from practice at the track?"

"Ron didn't ask me anything of the sort," she said, confused.

Sam hesitated. "I was going to mention it, but there were more interesting things to discuss."

"Were you simply getting me out of the way?" The tinge of hurt in her voice stung more than he would have anticipated.

"No, not at all." This looked bad, really bad. "I asked you to go because I enjoy your company and thought you might like to get out of the condo. I did intend to mention Ron's request that you refrain from attending practice when he works with Michael. He feels it distracts Michael and he wants him totally focused."

Tess crossed her arms. "We had an agreement, Sam. I'm here as Michael's chaperone and adviser. If Ron doesn't like that fact, then maybe he's not the best person to coach my son."

Michael leaned against the doorjamb. Sam suspected the kid had intentionally stirred up trouble to put a wedge between them.

"I happen to agree with Ron on this point. But how about if we meet with him tomorrow and we'll all sit down and discuss it?"

"At the very least, I don't like someone going behind my back. If Ron has a problem with me, he needs to come directly to me. The same goes with you, Sam."

Sam raised his hands. "I've tried to be very direct, but I didn't want to spoil our day—I was having too good a time. I apologize."

Tess held his gaze. "I don't like surprises. I much prefer knowing what I'm up against."

"I can't blame you for that. I'm the same way. Tomorrow, we talk to Ron and get some guidelines hammered out."

The strain eased from her stance. "Okay. Good night, Sam."

"Good night, Tess," he murmured. As an afterthought, he added, "Good night, Michael."

Sam whistled as he walked back to his truck. Until, that is, he heard the door behind him shut more forcefully than was necessary.

He suspected Michael McIntyre had issues with his mother having a social life.

Question was, did Sam want to see Tess in a romantic way badly enough to challenge Michael? And possibly lose the best rookie driver he'd seen in a long, long time?

CHAPTER NINE

TESS AND MICHAEL ARRIVED at Sam's office ten minutes before their arranged time.

The receptionist smiled at Michael. "It's good to see you again, Michael, Tess. I'll let Sam know you're here. Ron's already back there."

It shouldn't have surprised her that Ron was meeting with Sam ahead of them, but it made her uneasy nonetheless.

"Come on back—he's ready for you."

Tess and Michael went to Sam's office.

"Michael, Tess, glad you could come. Would you like anything to drink?"

They both declined.

Sam ushered them to the grouping of couch and chairs.

Tess glanced sideways at Michael, who couldn't seem to sit still.

She felt like the lone holdout at the Testosterone Club. Raising her chin, she refused to be intimidated. She'd worked with litigators who made these guys looks like kindergartners ready for story time.

The thought made her smile, releasing the tenseness. Business was business and racing was no different.

"I thought we might start by having Ron share plans for getting Michael ready to race in the NASCAR Busch Series."

Ron leaned forward. "We've got our work cut out for us if we're to have Michael ready to compete at that level by February. Not only compete, but win races." He handed each of them a bound report. "These are my recommendations for training and physical conditioning. As you will note, it's a very demanding schedule."

Tess paged through the document. "Yes, it is. He'll barely have time to sleep."

"He's young—he can handle it."

Taking a deep breath, Tess tried to avoid a knee-jerk reaction to Ron's brash statement. "Is it really necessary to work him twelve hours a day?"

Ron straightened, folding his arms over his chest. "I've been in this business for twenty-five years. I know the ins and outs and I'm considered one of the best crew chiefs, especially for a driver needing extensive training."

Tess nodded. "I certainly can't dispute that."

"What Ron is trying to say is that it'll be a challenge to get Michael ready in time. It will take tremendous dedication from both Michael and Ron. We need to do all we can to support them."

Sam obviously had his mediator hat on, which was fine with Tess. She had no intention of giving ground on important issues no matter the approach.

"I will support my son any way I can. But if I see a potential problem, I will also discuss that, too."

Ron leaned forward. "No offense, ma'am, but you

don't know anything about stock car racing. Sam's bent over backward to humor you, but I'm not going to do the same. It's time Michael grew up and was no longer tied to his mama's apron strings."

"Tess, what he means—"

She raised her hand. "He seems to be fairly articulate in expressing himself, Sam. You don't need to interpret for me."

Tess knew a power play when she saw one. "Ron, how do you propose for Michael to stand on his own two feet?"

"You go home to Phoenix."

"That's not an option. What's your Plan B?"

"You find a place to live off-site. Michael stays at the condo."

"Also not an option."

"Then I won't take on Michael," Ron said.

She stood. "Sam, I'd like to thank you for your faith in Michael and the time and money you've invested in him. However, I won't be able to agree to these terms."

"Tess, please sit down. I brought you two here today so you could work out a compromise."

"I see very little compromise in Ron's attitude."

Ron's eyes narrowed. "And you're just bent on keeping that boy tied to your apron strings. He's a grown man, for goodness' sakes."

Sam jumped in before Tess could tell the crew chief what she thought of him. "Ron, didn't you say it might be beneficial if Michael practiced without distractions?"

"Yeah."

"Tess, do you really feel it's necessary for you to attend home practices?"

"No, I suppose not." Judging from Ron's schedule, Michael would be spending way more time at the track than she cared to.

"So we've got a starting point. Ron, Michael is all yours during training time. His living arrangements remain the same."

"I guess it'll have to do," Ron said.

It stung to be all but banished from the track. For some reason, it would have meant a lot to know Sam was in her corner one hundred percent. But Tess was also a bit relieved not to be there morning, noon and night. She found racing intriguing, but not *that* intriguing.

"I'll give it a try," she agreed.

"What about me? Doesn't anyone care what I think?" Michael asked.

Ron raised an eyebrow.

Tess flushed. She'd forgotten about Michael in her quest to hold her own with Ron. "I'm sorry for talking about you as if you weren't here."

Ron snorted.

"What?" she demanded.

"That's just the kind of mollycoddling I'm talking about. It doesn't matter what Michael thinks. If he wants to win, he does what I say."

Tess held on to her temper. Barely.

"That's enough, Ron," Sam said. "You know I don't run that kind of team. I want my drivers to think for themselves."

Ron glared at Sam, then looked away.

Sam continued, "That said, I think we'll all agree

that, although he's made great strides and shows tremendous potential, Michael is still a green driver."

Tess nodded stiffly.

"I know I'm green," Michael's gaze was level. "And it's probably time I started learning some things on my own without my mom by my side most of the time."

Ron nodded, his expression relaxed.

Tess expected a pang of loss but only felt unsettled about one more shift in their relationship. *Change is good,* she reminded herself.

Michael straightened in his seat, his expression uncharacteristically grim. "But I want to make one thing perfectly clear. I respect my mother's opinion and I expect the people I work with to respect her, too. If that's not possible, it's time for me to walk away."

"Not a problem," Sam said. "I respect Tess immensely. Ron?"

Ron hesitated. "I wouldn't disrespect a woman. The track's still off-limits during practice."

"I can live with that." And their uneasy truce was reached.

TESS SORTED through canned goods to put in food boxes. She would have preferred the literacy program, but they'd needed a more long-term commitment. The food bank was the perfect solution.

Sam's presence as he worked right alongside her came as a surprise.

"Why didn't you tell me you volunteered so much here?" she asked.

"Didn't want you to feel obligated to choose the

food bank. Besides, the literacy thing seemed right up your alley."

"You've been doing this for a while, haven't you?" She nodded toward the two boxes he filled at the same time.

"Yeah. It's easy once you get used to the system."

Tess shook her head. "I doubt I'll be as gifted as you, but I'll give it a shot."

They worked silently for a few minutes. Tess found the repetitive work soothing.

"How are things working out with Ron?" he asked.

"Okay, so far. I've stayed out of his way this week and he's stayed out of mine."

"He's very good at what he does."

"I'm sure he is."

"But you don't like him?"

"No, I don't. But it doesn't matter whether I like him. If he works well with Michael, I'll ignore my personal feelings."

"What does Michael say?"

"Not much. Except that Ron's tough, but fair."

"That's pretty much my impression. It's going to be a challenge to get Michael ready in time for the Busch Series. Ron says the first month is going to seem a little like boot camp."

"I know Michael's exhausted. But I'm trying not to interfere. I just hope he'll speak up if Ron gets too aggressive with his training."

"None of us wants that. He did have a valid point, though. I'd be a fool if I didn't listen to his opinion."

What about my opinion?

Tess tried not to let it get to her. It shouldn't matter.

"I suppose." She sorted through the canned goods. "I'm really grateful to have somewhere to go these mornings. I'm not used to the life of leisure."

"And I'm glad to have some company filling these boxes. There will be more volunteers when we get closer to Christmas. Thanksgiving Day itself is always big for volunteering, too."

"I can't believe Thanksgiving's just around the corner."

"Are you and Michael going to Phoenix for the holidays?"

"No. My parents have developed a Thanksgiving cruise tradition, so there's no one to spend it with." Tess suppressed a pang of longing. "How about you?"

"Thanksgiving is usually with my folks in Chicago. They always have a full house, including my kids."

"I've always thought that kind of holiday sounded great. A large, extended family."

"It is great for the most part. A little too much family after a couple days, though."

"How come?"

Sam picked up his boxes and stacked them along the wall. When hers were finished, he did the same with her boxes. She wondered if he might ignore her question completely.

"I've never really analyzed the reason. Just knew I had to get out of there after a day or two…" He began filling a box, frowning in concentration.

That's how Tess knew he was mulling over the whole family thing. He normally effortlessly filled two boxes at a time.

She continued working and forced herself not to jump in and start asking more questions.

Finally, he said, "I guess it's because my folks have certain expectations of me. I'm the rebellious one who tossed aside my place in the family construction business on a whim. They'll probably always see me that way."

"And you see it differently."

His grin was crooked, his eyes shadowed. "Yeah, I saw it as finally taking control of my life. Doing what was right for me—I was much more drawn to real-estate investments and then to NASCAR. It had nothing to do with them."

"Surely they're proud of what you've accomplished."

"Yes, they're proud. But I also get the feeling they would have preferred me to be moderately successful in the family business than wildly successful in an unfamiliar area."

Tess's neck and shoulders tensed. She tried to tell herself it was from the repetitive motion, but she suspected it was more from Sam's story. Because it had a familiar ring.

She cleared her throat, desperate to change the subject. "You surprise me, Sam."

"Oh?"

"I expected you to be different. I guess I figured you'd be a hard-core adrenaline junkie, obsessed with racing to the point of excluding all else. And here you are, the owner of a successful company, assembling food boxes for the homeless. And going antiquing with me. Just not what I expected."

He studied her for a moment, then said, "I have my moments of tunnel vision. But usually there's just too much in life to see and do. Don't get me wrong—I love NASCAR. Always will. But there's more to life than just racing."

She gasped in mock horror. "Say it ain't so."

"Maybe I'll show you someday."

Awareness snapped and crackled in the air between them, sending Tess's pulse leaping. Truth be told, she didn't know if her reaction was anticipation at Sam's promise or relief at heading off a conversation that struck entirely too close to home.

MICHAEL WAITED for the green flag to drop along with the butterflies in his stomach. Even the NASCAR stars said that pretty much never changed.

He had pole position at a regional track somewhere in Georgia; he wasn't even sure where. His life had become a whirlwind of nonstop training and practice. By Thursday evening or Friday morning, he just got on the plane and went wherever Ron and Sam told him to go.

The flag dropped and Michael went into action, his movements smooth and sure. He took the lead from pole position and never relinquished it.

He had hoped somebody would challenge him and his newfound insight. But it wasn't to be tonight.

The win was exciting, but not nearly as exciting as it had been racing last summer on the sly. Before Sam, before Ron and the top-notch equipment.

But the big rush would return when he made that leap

into NASCAR proper, bypassing the truck series to run in the NASCAR Busch Series.

After his victory lap and pictures with the local media, he found his mother and Sam atop the motor home Sam had rented to be Kincaid Central. It made it easier for Sam to run interference between Ron and his mom.

Climbing the ladder, Michael was uncharacteristically irritated by what he saw when he stepped onto the roof. Sam and his mother sat side by side in lawn chairs. Sam leaned close to say something, and his mother laughed in response.

Michael was tempted to wedge himself between their chairs, but resisted the childish urge. According to Ron, he was maturing. Most days, he would agree. Except maybe where his mother and men were concerned.

His mom glanced up. "Michael, wonderful race."

He pulled up a chair on her other side. "Another win."

"You're doing great, son," Sam said.

"Thanks." *And don't call me son. I already have a father, working somewhere in Russia.*

"They couldn't catch you tonight," Sam commented. "Ron's doing some good work with you."

"Yeah, I'm learning a lot."

"It shows." His mom smiled and patted him on the arm. He shifted in his chair.

"Am I going to be up against the same drivers tomorrow night?"

"Probably. Why?"

Michael didn't want to sound ungrateful or as if he was getting full of himself. "It, um, just seemed kind of… easy."

Sam laughed. "And you wonder what the point is?"

"Kind of."

"You're right—these regional races are less and less of a challenge. Though, to be fair, you're driving the kind of equipment most of these guys only dream about."

"Yeah, I noticed." He felt like the rich, pampered kid attending an inner-city school. Only way safer.

"Tomorrow's going to be a pretty easy day. Maybe we can think of something the three of us can do," Sam suggested.

"I'd absolutely love to spend some time with my number-one son," his mom said.

His gut ached at the thought of all those times they'd shared when things had been so easy. No Ron pushing him to the end of his endurance. And no Sam hitting on his mom. Because Michael had no illusions about where all this nice stuff was headed.

Shrugging, he said, "I guess."

"Maybe we could try bowling?" his mom asked.

Michael snickered, until he realized she was serious. He so could not imagine his mom bowling. "Yeah, whatever."

"Unless, of course, you'd rather practice?" Tess asked. "I don't want to stand between you and practice."

"Nah, but I'll have to check with Ron first."

"Good, we'll plan on lunch and bowling, then?" Sam leaned close to Tess again.

"Sure." No way was he going to leave those two alone together all day. But, come to think of it, they spent time together during the week when he was training. Volunteering at the food bank and stuff like that.

If his mom was any less a straight shooter than she was, he might wonder if they were having an affair. But she'd always been up-front with him when she'd dated.

Catching Sam staring at his mom, Michael figured it wasn't for lack of interest on Sam's part. He wondered if she knew. She was so often oblivious to this kind of thing.

Michael certainly had no intention of enlightening her. Better to let sleeping dogs lie.

CHAPTER TEN

IT TURNED OUT to be quite a while before they were able to arrange an outing for just the three of them. As it was, they practically had to shanghai Michael from beneath Ron's nose.

"I'm afraid I'm violating the no-moms rule at practice." Tess raised her chin. It was the first time she'd been at the Charlotte track in a while.

"This isn't a practice. They're just testing out some changes on the car. Besides, you're with me." Sam wrapped his arm around her shoulder.

He'd been making gestures like that lately. And Tess had taken to touching his shoulder to make a point or tucking her arm through his as they walked. Nothing overtly sexual, just…friendly.

"Oh, that makes me feel so much better. I'm only accepted at practice if I'm sucking up to the boss."

"I see your point. Ron can be…tactless. But he gets the job done and I specifically made him available for Michael by shifting personnel."

Tess answered noncommittally. She didn't want to sound like a whiny, overprotective mother. But the truth was that she didn't dare to so much as leave a text message for Michael, for fear of getting him in trouble.

She missed her son, pure and simple. He'd been such a part of her everyday life and then all of the sudden he was gone—poof!

Ron glared at them from where he stood talking to Michael.

Michael shrugged and headed toward them, grinning. "Hey, Mom, Sam, I'm ready."

"Come on, let's go." Before the vile taskmaster changed his mind.

They left and had a relaxing lunch at Sam's favorite restaurant. Michael laughed and joked almost like his old self, keeping them entertained with his stories.

It made Tess happy in a bittersweet way, knowing there were probably very few of these moments on the horizon. And she suspected she hadn't fully appreciated them when they were plentiful.

When they arrived at the bowling alley, they found several bowling leagues lined up. Fortunately, Sam had reserved a lane.

She eyed Sam. "I still don't believe you bowl. And I really don't believe you rent shoes."

He touched the small of her back as he guided her to the shoe-rental counter. "Why's that so hard to buy?"

"Because—"

Michael interrupted. "Because, according to stuff I pulled up on the Internet, you're totally loaded."

"Michael!"

Sam laughed. "I'm comfortable, okay?"

They gave their shoe sizes to the clerk and changed shoes at one of the tables behind their lane.

"How long has it been since you bowled?" Sam asked.

"Not since high school. Michael's bowled quite a bit, though."

"That's okay, Mom, we'll help you out."

"Maybe, maybe not. We'll see. You're not the only one in the family with a competitive streak."

"That sounds like a challenge. Let's get this game going."

Tess found Sam's excitement contagious. He turned out to be a proficient bowler—no surprise there. And Michael held his own, though he threw an occasional gutter ball.

And Tess started out slowly, but caught on through dogged determination.

When Michael teased her, she responded, "Hey, I was rusty."

"You made a valiant comeback." Was that admiration she detected in Sam's voice? It amazed her that he wanted to spend his free time with them.

Two teenage girls in the next lane eyed Michael and giggled.

His frown of concentration told her he hadn't heard the girls discussing how cute he was. Good, he didn't need that kind of distraction. But glancing at Sam, she remembered a time when she'd been young, carefree and discovering the opposite sex. It had been a magical time. Before she'd realized the consequences of throwing caution to the wind.

Michael kept his gaze on the pins as he stepped forward and released the ball, knocking down all but one pin.

Tess and Sam congratulated him while the girls in the next lane giggled and cheered.

Michael turned toward the girls and grinned. It wasn't his usual shy smile. It was the confident smile of a man who knows he deserves the attention.

Tess sucked in a breath. It was the same smile that had drawn her to his wildly attractive and unattainable father.

She caught Sam's eye and he shrugged, as if to say, "What can you do?"

Michael went over to talk to the girls without waiting for the ball return. Sam had to remind him when it was time for his second turn. Michael threw the ball almost as an afterthought, already on his way back over to chat up the girls before all the pins fell. He didn't even turn to see what he'd scored.

Sam stepped close to Tess. "Looks like he's got another kind of scoring on his mind."

"That's what I'm afraid of."

"Wait till he gets to the big time. There are going to be girls throwing themselves at him all over the place."

Tess shook off the overwhelming urge to grab her son's hand and drag him out of the bowling alley and back to Phoenix, where his gifts didn't seem to garner the same attention.

"He's changed," she murmured.

"Yes, he has. It was bound to happen eventually, even if he'd gone to Stanford."

"Not this quickly, though. He needs time to adjust."

"Looks like he's adjusted fine. Maybe it's you who needs time to adjust." Sam's voice was gentle, understanding.

"Possibly."

"Don't tell me he's never had a girlfriend before."

"Oh, he had girls he liked. But they all hung around together in a big group. Nothing one-on-one." Tess flushed. "I mean nothing where he might jeopardize his future by doing something dumb."

"You sound like you speak from experience. I have a hard time visualizing you doing anything risky, even as a teen."

"Oh, if only you knew."

"Try me."

"I was a different person then—willing to take risks, sure that the future held all sorts of good things. When I met Royce in high school, he was so good-looking and fun, I just knew he was one of those good things." She shrugged. "It turned out to be the same old tired story. Girl falls in love with boy, girl gets pregnant, two kids get married way too young. The things that attracted me to Royce didn't make him such a great bet for marriage and fatherhood. Especially at eighteen."

"Mine is a variation of that story. Only my ex and I had a pretty good life for many years. But we eventually grew apart, and when the kids got to college, we realized there wasn't anything left. It was hard saying goodbye to someone who had been such a part of my life for so many years. But I knew we both deserved better. My ex-wife agreed. All very civilized and amicable."

There was a wistfulness in his voice that told her the breakup of his marriage hurt more than he was willing to admit.

She said, "I don't want my son to make the same mistakes I did."

"We all hope our kids make better choices than we did. Too bad they don't always listen." He shook his head, as if to dislodge poignant memories. "Let's finish up our game and get back to the track. Lover boy here has a race tonight."

Tess touched his arm, wanting to lighten his mood. "There is a bright side to racing. Between practice, training and racing, he won't have time to be alone with a girl. At least until he's, say, forty?"

Sam's chuckle warmed her heart.

Tess nudged him with her elbow. "A mother can dream, can't she?"

THE RACE that evening went much the same as the night before. The hair on the back of Sam's neck prickled when he watched Michael race. No doubt about it—Michael McIntyre would put Kincaid Racing on the map. They might be a bit of an underdog now, but give Michael a year in the NASCAR Busch Series and he'd be ready to tackle Cup contention.

As much as Sam liked to pretend that he owned a NASCAR team as a hobby, he was as competitive as the next guy. And, after so many years in the business sector, turning a profit was still his goal. Tax write-offs certainly weren't as satisfying.

He went down to the pits after the race, taking Tess with him. He felt her tense as they approached Michael and Ron.

Sam clapped Michael on the shoulder. "Good race."

"Thanks." Michael's face flushed. There was an awkward silence.

"Good race, honey." Tess stepped forward, kissing him on the cheek. Michael stiffened.

Tess drew back. "What's wrong?"

"Nothing."

"We'll need to practice tomorrow," Ron said, his tone terse.

"But tomorrow's Sunday," Tess protested.

"Sunday's a race day in NASCAR. Get used to it."

"Ron," Sam warned. He didn't like Ron treating Tess with borderline rudeness, but he had to admit the man's approach with Michael had worked wonders. Some space between mother and son had apparently been a good tactic.

"Sorry." But Ron looked anything but sorry. "Michael's going to need more practice until he overcomes that selective hearing."

Michael shrugged. "The radio was cutting out."

"Bull. You heard me loud and clear. You did what you wanted to do, not what I told you."

"I won, didn't I?" Michael's jaw clenched.

"Doesn't matter. You've got to trust my opinion and training. Cowboying it isn't going to work in the long run. You lucked out tonight."

"I was able to tell the wind shifted. By calculating the—"

"You don't need to calculate anything. You need to do what you're told."

Tess opened her mouth to speak, but Sam slid his arm around her waist and propelled her away. "Michael, you can meet us at the motor home when you get this all worked out."

Glancing over her shoulder, Tess frowned. "I think I should stay. Michael needs an advocate."

"Michael might need a good butt chewing. If he and Ron are working together, he's going to have to trust Ron's judgment. And when he proves he's capable, Ron will allow him more input."

"I don't like his approach."

Sam touched the small of her back, steering her through the crowd. He didn't try to soften his words. Tess needed to know where she stood in the scheme of things. And if he didn't support Ron in this, he might as well start looking for a new crew chief. "Doesn't matter if you agree with his approach. Like anything else, there's a hierarchy to racing. Michael needs to learn his place."

And so did Tess.

He felt Tess stiffen. Her words had a bite to them when she said, "As the driver, shouldn't he be making the decisions?"

"Maybe someday when he's seasoned. But he's young and green and needs to learn from the folks who have been around awhile."

"I'm sure if Ron would only sit down and explain why he wants Michael to do something a certain way, Michael would understand and comply."

"He doesn't have time, Tess. When they're out there racing at 180 miles per hour, split-second decisions are essential. The crew chief has information available that drivers don't have. Information from other guys on the team, computer calculations, things like that."

"Are you aware that Michael can calculate a lot of this in his head, as fast or faster than it takes for Ron to relay the information on the radio."

"That quickly?"

"Yes. He's phenomenal. And I'm not just saying that because he's my son. As long as he's committed to racing, you might as well make full use of his gifts."

"I'll have to discuss that with Ron."

She stopped and touched his arm. "I'm not trying to be difficult. I'm trying to help. Michael's never been the kind of person who did well under somebody's thumb. He almost flunked fourth grade because the teacher didn't understand that Michael could do things other kids his age couldn't even imagine doing. Michael's not a thinking-inside-the-box person. You'll lose him if you don't allow him some latitude."

"And you're telling me this why? I thought you wanted him to quit racing."

"I do. I did. I mean, I'm not so sure anymore what's best. But Michael needs a fighting chance."

"I'll discuss it with Ron, but honestly, most of this is simply a driver and a chief settling into a new working relationship. It's almost like a marriage. There are bound to be tensions until they find a balance that works."

Tess hesitated. "I guess that makes sense. Thanks for listening to my concerns. And thanks for explaining."

"Hey, I tend to forget this is a whole new world for you."

"It's definitely different than personal-injury law. But then again, people are people and sometimes it's best to listen even if you think you have all the answers."

"Exactly."

"I'll try to stay out of the thing with Ron and Michael as much as possible."

Sam sighed with relief.

SAM ENDED the phone call with his mother and looked out the large picture window. The lush landscape outside his office failed to soothe him as it normally did.

He felt pulled in too many directions these days. His mom and dad had opted out of the traditional Thanksgiving dinner held at their house to reunite with a college friend in Florida. The friend was terminally ill, so the gesture was kind and necessary, even if it did mess up his Thanksgiving plans.

His kids already knew about the change and had decided to spend the holiday at their mother's house. And, though she'd issued an invitation for him through the kids, he didn't feel comfortable hanging around for a long weekend. Her second husband seemed like an okay guy, but it wasn't Sam's idea of a relaxing holiday.

His watch alarm went off, reminding him it was time to leave for the food bank. He smiled, anticipating seeing Tess.

She was waiting out front when he arrived. "Hey, Sam." She grasped his hands and kissed him on the cheek. Her scent washed over him, something sweet and spicy and all Tess.

They put on aprons and latex gloves and started loading food boxes.

"How's Michael handling his regimen?" he asked.

"It *is* a little like boot camp. Where he was once

dragging his rear, he now barely complains. I'm seeing a new maturity in him."

"Good. I knew he was up to the challenge."

"I'm glad you did, because I was seriously worried there for a while."

He was glad to see her frown erased. "I know you were. It's good to see you relax, take things less seriously."

"I wasn't always serious, believe it or not." Tess smiled. "Motherhood kind of changed that. I was so young, I was scared I'd do something to really mess Michael up. It only got worse after Royce left...I guess I'll never be one of those hands-off kind of moms."

"You've done a terrific job of letting go. I bet Michael has no idea how hard it's been for you."

"I hope not. I don't want him to worry about me."

They worked in silence for a few minutes.

Tess cleared her throat. "His father called him the other night."

"That's a good thing, right?"

"Yes, except Royce started telling Michael how to handle Ron and to demand another crew chief if it doesn't work out. I think Michael kind of resented it. And to be honest, so did I. It's awfully easy to give armchair advice a continent away."

"Hey, Royce could have been giving you the excuse you needed to raise heck with Ron. I'm really glad you didn't."

"I suppose you're right. But I'd started to see the progress Michael was making."

Sam was relieved hearing Tess talk about her ex

like that. There didn't seem to be any residual romantic feelings. "Has Royce been around much with fatherly advice?"

"That's just it—he hasn't. It's as if this is some way for him to vicariously live through Michael."

"Ah, so the racing lessons for Michael were all tied up in that?"

"Exactly. But it's seemed to work out for Michael. He loves the driving, loves the lifestyle. He's even starting to grudgingly admit Ron's right a lot of the time."

"How about you?"

"I may not agree with everything he does or even particularly like the man. But I have to respect the results he's getting."

"Ron's not that bad once you get to know him."

"I'm not sure that'll ever happen. Something about me seems to push his buttons. I don't intentionally antagonize him."

"I know you don't. It is out of character, though."

"Is he married?"

Her question caught him by surprise. "He's divorced. Why?"

"Do they have children?"

"Grown now. The wife got custody and rarely allowed Ron to see them. He feels like she turned them against him."

"Ahh, now I see. Maybe I remind him of her in some way?"

Sam shrugged. "It's possible. He hasn't said anything to you, has he?"

"No, he barely speaks to me. Just glares. That's about it."

"Not much I can do about that."

"I'll survive. We've had clients who acted like that. I learned to shrug it off."

"I imagine people can get pretty nasty when they've been in an accident."

Tess nodded. "Most are grateful for my help. But a few have a chip on their shoulders before the accident, and see this as their opportunity to spew poison. The system very rarely works as quickly as they think it should."

"Probably not. Did you decide whether you're going to Phoenix for the holidays?" Sam told himself he was asking purely to have an idea of Michael's availability. But darn it, he enjoyed Tess's company. Was that a crime?

"I did. We're going to stay here in Charlotte. Have a quiet dinner together, then go view some of the sights. Poor Michael's barely seen anything but the track and the garage."

Sam tried not to smile at the news. An idea was forming. "How about you?"

"I manage excursions here and there. The racing schedule has been pretty intense."

"Just wait. It'll get more intense when we're racing in the Busch Series."

"Doesn't seem possible."

"You'll see." He only hoped Michael and Tess were both up to the challenge. Then again, Tess's six months would be up by then. Would she stay on?

Tess became quiet, apparently lost in thought, too.

Sam continued working. Finally, when he could stand the silence no longer he asked, "Something wrong?"

Shaking her head, she smiled sadly. "Just thinking this is such a different life from the one I'd envisioned for my son. I thought he'd get his degrees, teach or do research. Funny how life works out."

"Sounds like you're starting to accept racing as Michael's destiny."

"Maybe just trying on the idea for size."

"That's a step in the right direction." He sealed a box and added it to the stack lining the wall. "It looks like I'll be staying in Charlotte for Thanksgiving—my folks decided on visiting a friend in Florida and my kids are going to my ex's… I was wondering if you and Michael wanted to come over to my place for Thanksgiving dinner?" Sam held his breath. He felt as if he hadn't had so much riding on an invitation since senior prom.

Tess's smile beamed. "How thoughtful. That would be lovely, Sam. What should I bring?"

Everything.

Because he didn't know how to cook a turkey. Or much of anything else, for that matter.

CHAPTER ELEVEN

THE STANDS WERE FILLING rapidly around Tess and Sam. Another Saturday night at yet another dirt track.

Tess opened her needlework bag and removed her cross-stitch project. She was finishing a throw pillow for Michael depicting a racetrack scene. When she'd started, she told herself it would make a nice memento if he ended up at Stanford. Oh, who was she kidding? Still, it was hard to let go of her dream.

The next pillow on her list would be a Christmas present for Sam. She always tried to give something personal and handmade to the people she cared about. He was becoming a friend.

And maybe more? She hoped so, but he hadn't tried to kiss her again. Maybe tonight would be the night.

Tess pushed the thought from her mind. Still, she found herself smiling. She couldn't help but be impressed by the way Sam had forged ahead in life and done things his own way. And admire the way he'd given back to the community and taken Michael under his wing. And feel a little thrill of excitement when he seemed totally focused on her.

Glancing sideways, she caught Sam watching her, his smile bemused.

"What?" she asked.

"You're an intriguing dichotomy, Tess."

She chuckled. "And here I thought I was boring."

"Somewhat predictable at times, but never boring."

Wrinkling her nose, she said, "I'm not sure I like being considered predictable."

"Reliable?"

"Great. Now I sound like a used car."

"Then how would you describe yourself?"

"Hmm. I do what needs to be done. I take care of the people I love…."

"Who takes care of you?"

"Me? Nobody, really." The concept took her aback. "I guess I take care of myself."

"Not nearly enough. I know you've had a lot of responsibility raising Michael mostly on your own. Now you deserve to have some fun."

"I do have fun. I'm having fun right now."

"I got the feeling you were killing time."

Tilting her head, she considered his statement. Smiling guiltily, she said, "Yes, I guess I am. Truth be told, I could use a little less time at the races."

"Then do something else."

"And miss Michael race? No way. I have to be here for him."

"If Michael wasn't a concern and you could be anywhere else, where would you be on a Saturday night?"

Tess closed her eyes. It was a fantasy she hadn't contemplated in a long time. "I'd be in Venice, riding in a gondola. The night air would be cool and damp, with the music of a mandolin floating across the water."

She didn't tell him there was usually an unnamed man in the gondola with her. But tonight, she recognized him in her daydream. It was Sam.

She opened her eyes. "But that's probably not exciting enough for you."

"Why not? It sounds great."

"No horsepower, no loud engines, no competition."

Sam cupped her cheek with his hand. His eyes were dark and unreadable. "There's a time and a place for competition, Tess. And there's a time to savor the sweet things in life, slowly and completely."

Her cheeks warmed. The kind of savoring he mentioned was another of her fantasies.

He rubbed his thumb over her chin. Leaning closer, his breath was warm on her face. "Tess, you are one special lady. There's so much I'd like to show you."

Her needlework dropped from her hands. She wondered what to do with them now that they were idle.

Did he finally intend to kiss her again?

The noise of the crowds faded, as did the roar of the engines down in the garage. Tess could almost swear she heard the sweet strains of a violin concerto.

Sam's gaze dropped to her mouth.

Slowly, sweetly, he touched his lips to hers.

She could scarcely breathe, the moment was so fragile, yet so intense.

He nibbled her bottom lip, then drew away.

No, don't...

"I'm sorry, I probably shouldn't have done that."

...stop.

"It's fine." Tess almost rolled her eyes at her own ineptitude. How could a woman of thirty-seven be so dumb about seduction? "I mean, it was…nice."

Nice? Why couldn't she simply wrap her arms around him and show him exactly the kind of kisses she wanted from him? Hot, moist and provocative. The kind of kisses shared on gondolas and in the back seats of cars.

What the heck did she think she was doing, contemplating seduction with the owner of her son's team? But Sam was so much more than that.

Tess covered her confusion be leaning down to pick up her needlework. Brushing off imaginary dirt, she willed herself to quit acting like a breathless virgin. Even if, at times, she felt like one.

Turning to Sam, she touched his arm. When he glanced up, she met his gaze. "I'm not very good at this. What I'm trying to say is that I'd like to try this again sometime, when we have more of an idea what's happening with Michael. And when we can give each other the attention we both deserve."

Was that better?

It seemed to be, because Sam nodded slowly. A grin followed. "Sure thing. I'll hold you to that."

Tess hoped he would.

SAM TWINED his hand with Tess's.

She was the last woman he should consider getting involved with. And yet, there was something about her that made him want to take her to Venice and get her alone on a gondola. Then slowly remove her clothing, kissing every inch of her soft skin, and make love to her as the water lapped the side of the boat.

"The race is starting," she said.

"Huh?" In his fantasy she cried out in passion and the words definitely had nothing to do with a race.

She pointed to the track. "Michael's pole position again."

"Of course he is." Sam snapped out of his reverie. "He's by far the best driver out there. It's almost a waste of his time and talent."

"It's not a waste if he learns something while he's out there."

He wrapped his arm around her. "You can say that again."

The race started as usual, with Michael taking an immediate lead. Sam tried hard to keep focused on the race—something he normally did with ease. Especially where this phenomenal kid was concerned. But the phenomenal kid had a pretty phenomenal mother.

He was aware of Michael lapping the slower cars. Tess's sharply indrawn breath warned him something was wrong. That's when he saw one of the lapped cars try to stuff Michael's car into the wall. Michael's car got loose, the rear slewing on the high side.

"Come on, Michael. Get it under control," he murmured.

Tess's nails dug into his forearm.

Michael managed to avoid hitting the wall. But in his inexperience, he overcorrected and went into a spin. Two other cars piled into him before the yellow flag was thrown.

Tess stuffed her needlepoint into her canvas bag. Sam grasped her elbow and guided her down the stairs. "He should be fine, Tess. That car's designed to protect the driver through worse incidents than that."

She didn't answer, just walked faster. They made it into the pits as the tow truck brought in Michael's car.

Michael peeled back the window netting and levered himself out the window.

"Michael!" Tess went to his side before the EMTs had a chance to check him out.

"I'm okay, Mom. Not even a scratch." But the set to his jaw told Sam he was furious.

"You sure you're all right, kid?" Sam asked.

Michael nodded tersely.

Then a tow truck pulled in one of the other cars. The driver barely had time to exit the car and remove his helmet before Michael launched himself at the guy.

He swung, his fist connecting to jaw with a sickening crunch.

The other driver shook his head as if to clear it. Then swung at Michael.

Sam launched himself into the fray, trying to separate the two men. A stray punch connected with his eye. He grunted in pain.

Someone grabbed the other guy from behind and locked him in a bear hug. Sam pulled Michael away, cursing the whole while.

"Come on, kid, you need to cool off."

"I'm going to make that guy sorry we were on the same track."

"No, you won't. You'll shake it off and ignore him.

You may be mad as hell and rightfully so, but you will *not* retaliate. Do you understand?"

Michael's chest heaved as he struggled to catch his breath.

Slowly, the light of battle faded from his eyes. He gingerly touched his cheek where the other driver had landed a punch.

Only then did Sam glance at Tess. Her eyes were huge, and her lips trembled. Then she straightened her shoulders as if to do battle herself. "Michael Royce McIntyre, what is the meaning of this? I raised you better than to resolve your problems by violence. You're acting like a thug."

"Did you see what he did?" Michael demanded.

"Yes, I did. It was very unsportsmanlike. And I'm relieved that you're fine. But I do *not* condone fighting."

Michael's shoulders sagged. "I guess I screwed up."

Sam smothered a grin. "Only if you don't learn from it, son."

THE FLIGHT BACK to Charlotte the next morning started off as a silent affair.

Sam sported a shiner from his efforts in breaking up the fight, and Michael had a bruise on his cheek. And Tess wouldn't have been surprised if her hair had turned white overnight.

The race kept replaying in her mind, particularly the part where Michael's car started going sideways. It was in slow motion, prolonging her anxiety, even though she knew Michael was fine.

"This is exactly why I didn't want Michael to race,"

she commented. If she couldn't have any peace, why should they? "I had a perfectly intelligent, good-natured son before he came to Charlotte. Well, with the exception of wanting to throw away his education. After four months here, he's fighting and cursing and all sorts of things I probably don't know about. I swear you've turned into your father's son."

"Mom, this is the only time I've stepped out of line."

"Oh, and what about the underage drinking?"

"Okay, twice," Michael mumbled.

"And how many times did you get in trouble for drinking before you came here?" she asked.

"None." His tone was sullen.

"And how many fights?"

"None."

She turned to Sam. "And tell me how this is promoting his growth as a human being?"

"Please, no more." Sam raised his hand as if to ward off her words. He looked downright pathetic with his swollen eye. But not pathetic enough for her to let him off the hook.

"Oh, I haven't even begun. We've got an hour or more in flight and I intend to make good use of it."

Sam groaned.

"It won't do any good, man," Michael said. "She'll keep at it until she's run us into the ground."

Tess managed not to smile. Signs of weakness would only encourage them. And she wanted to make sure they were every bit as miserable as she had been last night watching her son's car careen out of control. Then watching her son try to beat another man to a pulp. Those were two things no mother should have to see.

"Michael, your behavior last night was inexcusable. I've never seen you lose your temper like that. They let you off easy with a fine," she said.

"And, Sam, I hold you partially responsible, too. Apparently you haven't taught Michael how to respond in these kinds of situations. It was bound to happen and he needs guidance. Perhaps you should discuss some sort of stress-reduction regimen with Ron. Or perhaps I should." It was an idle threat, but it elicited a satisfying groan from both men.

"I'm so angry I can barely look at you two. I'm going to read my book. I would suggest you rest up and contemplate how to make sure something like this doesn't happen again."

"Yes, ma'am," they said in unison.

CHAPTER TWELVE

SAM HAD MADE an effort to coordinate his volunteer time at the food bank to coincide with Tess's. But today, he wished he could avoid her.

She was already there when he arrived, assembling food boxes.

"Hi," he said.

"Hi." She barely glanced his way.

They worked in silence for a few moments, before he steeled himself to do what needed to be done. "I've given it a lot of thought and you were right. I should have prepared Michael more for aggressive drivers and keeping his cool in tense situations. I intend to remedy that ASAP."

"Thank you. It's hard for me to see him headed in a really wrong direction."

"We agree on that point. I've also been considering other things I can do to prepare him—things I might have overlooked because my drivers have generally had a little more experience under their belts. I also intend to prepare him for life in the public eye. How to handle himself with the media, pitfalls to avoid, that kind of thing."

"Yes, that should definitely be covered."

"And I'm making a sports psychologist available to him."

Tess's eyes widened. "Do you think he needs counseling?"

"Not now. But if he does as well as I think he will next year, he's going to get a whole lot of media attention. It could be a bumpy transition, and I want him to know there's someone he can talk to who will understand. I can't do that and neither can you, no matter how badly we want to try."

"Is it common practice for drivers to use a sports psychologist?"

"Some. Many just have a mentor or crew chief as a sounding board. If Michael and Ron had really hit it off, I probably wouldn't even suggest it. But the kid has to have some sort of outlet, some person he can trust to advise him."

"I've always been very open with Michael. I think he knows he can talk to me about anything."

"There are certain topics a guy just can't discuss with his mother. Like how to handle the women who are likely to throw themselves at him."

Tess smiled. "They should be throwing themselves at him now. He's very special."

"Exactly. It can mess with a guy's head when all of a sudden he's the flavor of the day because he drives NASCAR. Some people won't have his best interests at heart."

"And you're telling me this why? To make me even more nervous about his future? Or to give me another reason to pack him up and take him back to Phoenix?"

Sam stepped closer. "I know I'm taking a big chance in laying it all out there for you. I could lie and tell you we'll be able to protect him all the time. But I value your trust too much. Besides, you're too darn smart to fall for that."

"Right." She smiled.

He noticed the way her eyes crinkled and the slight dimple in her chin. Even in jeans and a T-shirt, with her hair drawn back in a ponytail, she had a serene beauty that other women couldn't imitate if they tried.

"So we're on the same page where Michael's concerned?" It was more important to him than he'd ever anticipated.

Tess nodded. "Sounds like it. I'm sorry for lecturing you yesterday on the plane. You're an adult and I treated you like a kid."

Cupping her cheek with his hand, he murmured, "You were scared."

Her eyes widened, her lips parted. "I was…not."

She started as one of the food bank employees dropped a carton of canned goods nearby.

"Thanks, buddy," Sam muttered under his breath. The moment was gone.

But his mood brightened when he realized there would be plenty more opportunities.

"I figured you and Michael could come over about one o'clock on Thursday. Maybe eat around two?"

"That's right, I nearly forgot Thanksgiving with everything that's been going on. What can I bring?"

"How are you at baking pies?"

"Pretty good, if I do say myself." Her eyes sparkled. "Pumpkin?"

"That'd be great."

"Anything else?"

"Nope, I've got it handled," Sam lied. For some reason, it was important that she view him as a hearth-and-home kind of guy. Able to cook, entertain and the more manly stuff besides. But, hey, he'd read somewhere a turkey could be roasted on a barbecue grill. What could be more manly than that?

TESS'S FIRST INKLING that all might not be well came when her phone rang at 10:00 a.m. on Thursday morning.

"Tess, it's Sam. I called my mom on her cell, but she didn't pick up. Probably walking on the beach."

She had a hard time keeping up with his rapid-fire logic. "Oh, yes, your folks are in Florida."

"Yeah, well, I've got a slight problem. When the instructions said to thaw the turkey in the fridge for three to four days, I thought they must be exaggerating. And I didn't want everyone to come down with salmonella, so I moved it from the freezer to the refrigerator Tuesday evening and—"

"It's still frozen."

"What do I do?" His voice contained an uncharacteristic note of panic. This was the man who negotiated complex real-estate deals without batting an eye?

"Fill the sink with cold water—"

"Yeah, I read that but it didn't make sense. Wouldn't hot water thaw it more quickly?"

"Remember salmonella?"

"Okay, cold it is. How quickly will it thaw?"

"It might take an hour or two…"

"But the instructions say it's going to take four hours to cook. I'd hoped to smoke it on the barbecue, but that would take even longer."

"Why don't we just plan on eating a little later? I don't mind."

"I've got some other people coming, too. Ron invited himself, and I didn't have the heart to say no. And Sally from the food bank will stop by after her shift. And a couple guys from the crew."

"Okay, give me an hour and I'll be over. We can do this."

"Thanks, Tess. I owe you big-time."

She woke Michael, who had been taking advantage of a rare morning to sleep in.

He squinted at her, shielding his eyes with his hand.

"Sam needs a little help with the food preparation. I'm going to leave in about half an hour. Do you want to come with me now or go at one by yourself?"

Collapsing back against his pillow, he pulled the covers over his head. "Later," he mumbled.

Tess smiled. It was good to see some things didn't change. Especially when everything else in life seemed to be in a state of flux.

She changed from her flannel pj bottoms and sweat-shirt into a pair of black slacks and purple blouse. The soft fabric draped nicely and made her feel feminine and desirable.

Or was it the thought of seeing Sam that made her feel that way?

Shaking her head, she refused to follow that line of thinking. Still, she took as much care with her hair and makeup as she could and still be out the door in half an hour. Grabbing the package of roasting bags from her cupboard, she headed toward Sam's house, following his directions carefully.

Tess let out a low whistle when she pulled into his circular drive. It was a beautiful old colonial, apparently lovingly restored. The grounds were beautiful, but not overly opulent—the overall effect was elegant, yet homey. She sighed with sheer envy.

Her envy evaporated when Sam answered the door. His usual unflappable demeanor was definitely flappable.

"Tess, thank goodness you're here." He grasped her hand and hauled her into the house.

"You sounded rather…desperate."

"I admit defeat." Sam led her through the great room to the kitchen. She had the vague impression of casual, comfortable furniture, but nothing to give the room personality. Nothing to make it feel like home.

They went through the arch and Tess stopped abruptly. Her jaw dropped. "Wow."

Sam shrugged. "The Realtor said it was a kitchen to die for. I guess it's got everything we need."

"It certainly does," she breathed. Top-of-the-line, commercial-grade appliances, a center island as big as some people's entire kitchen and gorgeous cookware hanging from wrought-iron hooks in the ceiling.

Tess went to the sink and poked the wrapped turkey with her finger. "It's still pretty frozen. This calls for an emergency thaw."

"I thought this *was* the emergency thaw."

"We take it one step further, immersing the un-wrapped turkey to thaw inside and out at the same time. Do you have bleach?"

"We're going to thaw it in bleach?"

"No, we're going to wipe down the sink to destroy any bacteria."

"Okay, you're the boss." Sam went to the pantry and returned with a bottle of bleach. He took out a towel and applied the bleach. "Like this?"

The antiseptic odor made her step back. "Yes. Then rinse and fill one side with cool water."

He complied. "Now what?"

"Wash your hands, unwrap the turkey…"

After he complied, she walked him through the quick-thaw process.

"Tell me something?"

"What?" he asked.

"You apparently have enough money to have this shindig catered, or at the very least buy everything premade at any number of restaurants. So why insist on cooking?"

He shrugged, his smile sheepish. "I was trying to impress you."

Tess was touched by his answer. And more than a little surprised. Most men who had money, and she had come into contact with quite a few at the law firm, thought the only way to impress a woman was by making a big show of throwing cash around.

"And why's that?" Her voice was softer than she intended, husky almost.

"Because I...I don't know."

He was up to his elbows in turkey carcass and had to be about the sexiest man she'd ever seen. His unorthodox approach was working. Or maybe it was simply because she really liked him and almost anything would have worked.

"Of all the women you could impress, why me?"

Glancing around in search of a quick exit, his gaze landed on the turkey, a mutant extension of his arm. He seemed to realize escape wasn't an option. Not without divesting himself of the raw bird and scrubbing his arms to the elbows.

"You're not going to let me get out of this gracefully, are you?"

Tess laughed. "Getting out gracefully wasn't an option pretty much the minute I stepped into the kitchen."

Shrugging, he said, "You fascinate me. That's the reason I wanted to impress you."

"That sounds rehearsed."

His face began to flush. "I'm at a disadvantage here. It's hard to come up with a good line while my hand is stuck up a— Never mind, you get the picture."

Tess held his gaze, willing him to say something sincere. "Why don't you forget about lines and just tell me the truth?"

"If I knew what it was, I *would* tell you." He seemed so genuinely baffled.

"You figured once I sampled your cooking, I'd give up all thoughts of dragging Michael back to Phoenix?"

"No, but come to think of it, it's not half-bad."

"Granted, I find a man who cooks very intriguing."

"You do?" Hope sparked in his eyes.

"Especially one who would go to all this trouble and is secure enough to risk falling flat on his face."

"Hey, I haven't tanked yet. I still have time."

"Yes, you do." She touched his arm and tentatively moved closer.

"Tess, you're smart and sexy and classy. You have an elegance of spirit that is so unusual these days." He closed his eyes as if to will himself elsewhere.

Tess wasn't a risk taker by nature, particularly in romance. But he was so obviously floundering that she closed the remaining space between them and placed her palms on his face, holding him captive.

Sam's eyes opened. She leaned in and kissed him, tentatively at first, then more intimately. She tried to show him in every way possible what she couldn't put into words.

His low moan made her smile against his lips. He moved as if to draw her close, then realized he was wearing a turkey carcass for an oven mitt.

Tess twined her arms around his neck and snuggled against him, savoring the warmth of his body against hers.

His chuckle reverberated against her ear, where he nibbled. "You don't play fair."

Tess tilted her head, inviting him to trail kisses down her neck. "No, but I tend to play for keeps," she murmured.

CHAPTER THIRTEEN

SAM FELT almost as if he were one of those old cartoon characters with steam billowing out his ears. He trapped Tess against the counter and returned her kiss. His self-control plummeted when she pressed her body close to his.

Tess murmured his name, parting her lips in invitation. Oh, how he wanted to make love with this woman. To take her upstairs to his bed, slowly remove her clothes to reveal her gorgeous body. And listen to her murmured endearments as he made love to her again and again.

He used his good arm to tuck her even closer, careful not to allow his sticky hand to come in direct contact with her back—she'd managed to make him nearly forget the turkey gore harbored there. And the dead weight immobilizing his numb right hand reminded him he served as a human turkey defroster.

She whispered his name, her breath warm against his cheek. Trailing kisses along his jawline, she nipped his earlobe.

His breath lodged in his chest, he couldn't seem to exhale.

"Sam?"

He realized, as if through a haze, her kisses had stopped. He opened his eyes.

"I asked what time your guests were arriving."

Damn.

"One," he croaked.

"Then we better get back down to business."

"By that, I hope you mean picking up where we left off? Like you said, I can always have a restaurant deliver the meal."

She smiled up at him, regret flashing in her eyes. "I thought there was a principle at stake here?"

"There are more pleasant ways I could impress you."

"Awfully confident, aren't you? I'm sorry if I gave you the wrong impression. I do find you attractive, turkey and all." She gestured at his arm, grinning wickedly. Suddenly her smile faded. "But I'm still not sure it's a good idea to get so involved with my son's boss."

Sam smothered a groan of frustration. There had been a time when he might have tried to convince her differently. But he knew in his heart she was right.

"I can accept that, I guess." It took a great deal of self-control to step away from her. Contemplating a second Mrs. Kincaid helped, though. He wasn't at all sure he was ready for that kind of commitment again. "Um, I think this bad boy is ready to go in the oven. See what you think?"

She frowned, eyeing him up and down.

"I meant the turkey."

Humor sparkled in her eyes. She looked absolutely lovely, absolutely kissable—and absolutely off-limits. For the time being.

MICHAEL SWORE under his breath. His mom was going to have his hide. He'd overslept and was nearly a half hour late.

Fortunately, he could get there faster than most. He geared down and expertly changed lanes to avoid slow-moving traffic. Glancing in the rearview mirror, the sight of red-and-blue flashing lights made his gut drop.

Pulling over to the shoulder, he put the car in Park and shut off the engine. He lowered his window and had his license and registration ready when the officer approached.

"Where's the fire?"

"No fire, sir."

"I mean, what's your hurry?"

"I'm, um, late for Thanksgiving dinner. My mom's going to have my hide."

"Hmm. There are lots of folks on the road who would like to get to their Thanksgiving dinners in one piece. And I'm sure your mama would like your hide to stay intact at least until you arrive. You've been tailgating, speeding and driving recklessly."

"You don't understand. I'm a NASCAR driver." Well, he would be in a couple more months.

"I wish I had a nickel for every time I've heard that one, kid."

"No, really." Surely the guy wouldn't give him a ticket. "I'm a member of Kincaid Racing."

The cop returned his license and registration. "I'm sure Mr. Kincaid will give you time off to contest your ticket in court, if you so choose. Otherwise, it's defensive-driving school for you."

"You're kidding. I was a star pupil at the Boyd School of Performance Driving and I've been training with Ron Waltham for the past couple months."

"You shouldn't have any problem passing defensive-driving class, then." He winked and handed him the ticket. "Slow down, drive safe and have a Happy Thanksgiving."

Michael raised his window and muttered a blue streak. His mom would have a canary. Unless she didn't know about it. Maybe he'd talk to Sam, man to man, and explain the situation. He was sure to understand.

Nodding, Michael felt a whole lot better. The world wouldn't end because of one speeding ticket.

When he reached Sam's house, he realized the world might not end because of a ticket, but it was tilting pretty good on its axis because his mom had obviously spent too much time alone with Sam. Her mussed hair and guilty expression made it look like more than turkey had been cooking in that kitchen.

TESS WAS RELIEVED when Michael arrived. "I've been worried about you, honey. Why didn't you answer your cell phone?"

"I...turned off the ringer. Sorry I'm late. I should have called."

"It would have saved me worry. Come on in. Lucky for you, dinner's going to be a little late."

Sam entered the great room to stand behind Tess. His palm was warm against her back. "Your mother's been worried sick, Michael."

Michael's chin came up, his eyes narrowed. He glanced pointedly at Sam's hand. "Yeah, I can tell."

Tess's cheeks warmed as she remembered kissing Sam in the kitchen. She tried to widen her eyes innocently. "What do you mean?"

He glared at her.

She met his gaze, forcing herself not to feel guilty. She and Sam were consenting adults. There was absolutely nothing to feel guilty about.

Other than the fact that Sam was Michael's boss and she'd managed to complicate an already complex situation.

"I didn't mean anything," Michael muttered. "It's just been a crummy morning, that's all."

Tess's heart went out to her son. Holidays were always difficult for him since he didn't have the average family. She suspected he still longed for his father to show up.

"Make yourself comfortable, honey. Sam's got a tray of appetizers I'll bring out."

Michael seemed somewhat mollified once he got food in his stomach.

And shortly thereafter, Ron and the other guys arrived. Tess stepped to the background as Sam welcomed them. The last impression she wanted to give was that of being the hostess. Wouldn't *that* sit well with Ron?

Fortunately, Ron got distracted by racing talk with

Michael and the other two men while she helped Sam set the table.

"You are a wonder, Tess. I couldn't have pulled it off without you," Sam murmured close to her ear.

She eased a step away, afraid Ron or Michael might notice their proximity. "You did fine once we got the bird thawed."

"Those cooking bags sure did the trick. I had no idea they shortened cooking time."

"Now you know my secret." She smiled up at him, thinking he had the most wonderful eyes. So intelligent and warm, yet with a hint of danger.

"I'd like to know all your secrets, Tess McIntyre."

Her pulse accelerated at his intimate tone. It shocked her to realize she hadn't felt this strongly about a man since she'd fallen in love with Royce, Michael's father.

The thought had her taking a giant step backward, putting a safe distance between them.

"I think everything's here, if you want to let the guys know dinner's ready," she said.

He hesitated, frowning slightly. "Yes, I think you're right."

Things went from tense to tenser as everyone took their seats. As luck would have it, Ron sat directly across from her. His glare indicated he wasn't any happier about it than she was.

But for the most part, conversation revolved around racing, and Tess let it wash over her as Sam carved the turkey.

"I'll be starting some training next week with Michael on the simulator," Sam said. "He needs some more work on evasive action and what to do when someone tries to stuff him into the wall."

"He's had enough time on the simulator," Ron replied. "He just needs to practice, listen and do what I say."

Tess didn't like Ron's dictatorial style, and it was getting harder and harder to bite her tongue. Taking a deep breath, she commented, "I've found Michael works better when he participates in the decision-making process."

"Thanks for sharing that." Ron's lip curled. Then he pointedly turned to Sam as if she didn't matter. "I'm telling you, Sam, you spend too much time on the simulator and all that boy's gonna be good for is playing at the arcade."

Sam opened his mouth—

"My mother's right. I should participate in the decision-making process. You all treat me as if I'm not even in the room. I'm an adult and I have pretty good ideas of my own every once in a while."

"Sure you do, kid." Ron might as well have patted him on the head.

"Here, Ron, looks like you could use some more turkey." Sam stood, grasped the platter and slid a slice of white meat onto Ron's plate. "Did I tell you I cooked it myself? I'm pretty proud of it, too. I discovered these things called cooking bags, big old plastic bags you cook the bird in. Can you believe it?"

"Yeah, I think my ex-wife used to cook our turkeys in those."

Tess could definitely understand why she was the

ex-Mrs. Waltham. Any woman in her right might would run as fast and as far as she could to get away from taciturn Ron.

John, one of the crew members, brightened. "My dad soaks ours in this brine stuff and cooks it in a smoker all day long. Man, is it good."

A discussion on the pros and cons of smoking versus deep frying commenced. She could have sworn Sam was enthralled, until he winked at her when no one was looking.

He was simply defusing a charged situation. Which made her wonder if he'd really been as helpless with that turkey as he'd led her to believe.

CHAPTER FOURTEEN

SAM GRINNED as Michael walked into the classroom. "Have I got a surprise for you, kid."

"You know, I'd appreciate it if you didn't call me kid. I'm at a disadvantage because of my age as it is."

Raising an eyebrow, Sam gathered up some books and handed them to Michael. "Sure thing. Didn't realize it was a sore spot. Here's some reading material to help prepare you for what you're up against. How rivalries sometimes come about, that kind of thing."

"Okay. But back to the kid thing, you need to understand I want to be taken seriously. I'm tired of everyone acting as if my opinion doesn't count."

"A lot of people think a driver's opinion doesn't count until he's got several winning seasons behind him. Kind of like putting your money where your mouth is."

"Are you one of those people?"

"Sometimes, yeah. But one of the things that impressed me about you from the very start is how smart you are. Not only book-smart, but you have a lot of common sense, too. You can thank your mother for that."

"She's always been there for me."

Sam nodded. "I guess I'd better ask your opinion about my plans for today. How would you like to go out and play? Not in a kid kind of way, though."

Michael shrugged, eyeing him suspiciously.

"Good. I've got a friend who has a private dirt track just out of town. I thought maybe you could play bumper cars with some friends of mine."

"Bumper cars?" Michael looked as if he thought Sam had gone crazy.

"Kind of a real-life simulation so you can learn how to react to someone trying to put you out of the race."

Michael grinned as realization dawned. "Kind of like demolition derby?"

"Exactly."

"Does my mom know?"

Sam hesitated. "I told her we were working on evasive action, but I didn't go into too much detail."

"Oh, lying through omission. I get it."

"Sometimes you're too darn smart for your own good."

"Yeah, I hear that a lot. Hey, Sam, can I ask you a favor?"

"Shoot."

"I'm gonna need a day off next month. I'll know by next week when it will be."

"What's going on?"

"I don't really want to tell you because it will put you in a bad position with my mom. More of that lying-through-omission stuff."

Wincing, Sam wished he'd been more up-front with

Tess about today's exercise. But not badly enough to call her at the food bank. "Why don't you let me be the judge of that?"

Michael sighed. "I got a speeding ticket on my way to your house Thanksgiving day."

Sam was relieved it was relatively minor trouble. Not like a court date for drug possession or DUI. "You've got to be more careful, Michael. Just because you drive 180 miles per hour on the track doesn't mean you can disobey the speed limit."

"I know, I know. I'll watch it from now on. But I need to go to defensive-driving school."

"Go do your time and keep your mouth shut. Today should be all the defensive driving you'll ever need, though." The offensive driving he'd pick up on his own.

"Cool. Sounds like fun."

"We'll have you strapped in so tight, you'll hardly feel a thing. It'll be very safe."

"Let's do it, then." He headed for the door. Turning, he asked, "You won't tell my mom about the ticket, will you?"

Sam hesitated. He hated keeping things from Tess. It would have been so much simpler if he'd hired a seasoned driver. "Not unless I feel it's absolutely necessary."

TESS WAS READING the newspaper, drinking her morning coffee when Michael emerged from his room. He was dressed, but definitely not ready for the day to begin.

"I'm concerned about you, Michael. You're hobbling

like an old man. Isn't Ron going a little overboard with your physical training?"

"I pushed a little too hard yesterday." He winced as he reached to pull out a chair at the dining-room table.

"I'll say so. Maybe you need to see a doctor."

"No, I'll limber up."

"Are you sure?"

"Very sure."

"You came in pretty late last night. How was your day yesterday?" Tess asked.

"Good. I learned more about evasive actions than I ever suspected existed."

"You'll definitely need defensive driving, from what I've seen."

He paled. "Defensive driving?"

"Yes, you know, how to avoid a collision. When you've got forty-three men going 180 miles per hour, somebody's eventually going to make a mistake."

Michael smirked. "Yeah, a mistake. Well, I gotta go. Ron's got a really full day for me today, since yesterday was bumper, um, Tuesday."

"What does Tuesday have to do with it?" She tore off a piece of bagel and popped it in her mouth.

"Just an extra busy day." He jumped up, groaning as he did. "Gotta go, Mom. See you later." He kissed her cheek and was gone.

Shaking her head, she thought racing had turned her son into a complex, confusing person. These days, she felt there was a vital piece of the puzzle missing. Maybe paying more attention to the ins and outs of the business would help her understand.

SAM WAS PLEASED when his administrative assistant told him Tess was there. "Hi, beautiful," he said as she entered his office.

And she was beautiful. Khaki slacks and a casual blouse, her hair pulled back with some sort of clip.

Her cheeks grew pink, but her smile was wide, telling him she liked flattery once in a while.

"I hope I'm not interrupting something."

"Not at all. If you'd been here two hours ago, I would have allowed you to shanghai me to lunch."

"If I'd have known, I would have definitely been here earlier."

Was she flirting with him? The ever-cautious Tess? But then again, she'd been anything but cautious when she'd kissed him the other night. His pulse thrummed at the very thought.

Smiling, he reminded himself to take things slowly. "You're here now—that's what counts. Have a seat."

It felt awkward having Tess seated on the other side of his desk. As if forcing an all-business relationship when they were well beyond that, if only as friends.

"I feel like I don't know my son anymore. I want to learn more about racing, so I can understand everything he's going through."

Sam nodded. "I'll help if I can. What do you want to know?"

"I've read a few of the books you sent home for Michael to read. And I checked out a few more at the library."

"The best way to really learn is to hang out at the

track. And find a few dedicated fans willing to share their expertise."

"Michael says his schedule will be easier in December?"

"Yes. The off-season. It allows everyone to have some time with family at the holidays."

Tess grew pensive. "I think we'll stay in Charlotte for Christmas. My house is rented, so we'd have to stay in a hotel. Besides, the condo is almost starting to feel like home."

Sam was pleased that she seemed to be settling in. His plans to ship her back to Arizona ASAP seemed to have evaporated somewhere along the line. He found he missed their conversations when he didn't see her for a day or two. Missed *her*, in fact.

"My kids are flying in Christmas Eve, flying out December 26. So I'll have some extra time on my hands if you'd like the Sam Kincaid crash course on stock-car racing, no pun intended." The offer was out before he remembered they weren't supposed to be getting involved. But did that mean they couldn't spend time together? He thought not.

"That's wonderful. I don't want to keep you from your kids, though, should they decide to stay longer."

"They won't. Andrew and Stephanie have very busy lives, and that's about all the time they can spare for their old man."

"Ah, do I detect a bit of empty-nest syndrome?"

"Could be. For years and years their lives revolved around me and my ex-wife, and then one day, I looked up and they were gone. Didn't need me anymore." He aligned his desk blotter with the edge, unable to meet her eyes. "It might be one of the reasons I enjoy having Michael on my team."

"Stealing my son to replace yours?" Her smile took the edge off her question.

All the same, her teasing hit a nerve. Was that what he'd done?

"No, I wouldn't consider stealing your son. I might borrow him, though, if you don't mind."

She inclined her head. "I'll consider loaning him to you. On one condition."

"What's that?"

"You ask Ron to ease off on the training on Tuesdays."

"Why Tuesdays?"

"Because Michael says they're especially tough. And the poor boy was so sore this morning he could barely move."

Sam felt a pang of guilt. He might as well come clean. "Yesterday he had more than his regular workout—he had evasive-action training. Or, as I refer to it, bumper cars."

Tess's smile faltered. "That sounds pretty benign. Is it?"

"It depends on your definition of benign. Necessary? Absolutely. But it wouldn't surprised me if Michael is a bit bruised and sore."

Crossing her arms, she asked, "And why is that?"

"Because bumper cars is kind of like the old-time demolition derby, with modern safety features. It involved Michael driving on a track with a few of my old racing buddies. They practiced some aggressive moves on Michael and he learned ways to avoid them and control his vehicle."

"So these guys were out there trying to run Michael into the wall?"

Sam nodded. "Or spin him out, like what happened at his last dirt-track race."

"Is it safe?"

"Yes. He has the same protective measures as when he's racing. It's not uncommon to feel a little banged up by the end of the day, though."

"Why didn't you tell me this was what he would be doing?"

"Because I was afraid you might…"

"Freak out?"

"Exactly."

"And Michael was okay with this? He wasn't scared? You forget I specialize in personal-injury cases—car accidents. I've seen the damage an accident can do to a person's body."

"I think if you'll ask Michael, he'll be the first to tell you he had a blast. Sure, it's kind of unsettling to get hit the first time, but after a while, it's like a bunch of kids playing bumper cars."

"He wasn't having fun this morning." She started to rise. "I better get him in to see a doctor."

Sam held up his hand. "Tess, wait. He's fine. I had a sports trainer out there with us and he checked him after the race. He's probably bruised from the restraint system and that's about it."

"I know how serious soft-tissue injuries can sometimes be. A person can feel fine right after an accident and then several days later, they're barely able to walk."

"Tess, I don't think a doctor is necessary. Michael's young and physically fit—he can handle it. This is much less punishment on the body than a football player endures week in, week out."

She crossed her arms over her chest. "I wasn't too wild about him playing football, either."

"The last thing I want to do is see Michael get hurt. That's why we have these exercises. They ultimately result in a safer driver."

"I still intend to keep an eye on him. If he's not better in a couple days, I'm taking him to the doctor. Sports trainer or no sports trainer."

"Agreed." Sam pulled out his desk file drawer and removed a thick bound document. "As for learning more about racing, you can start with this. NASCAR rules and regulations."

Tess's eyes widened. "All *this?*"

"Yes, and they change quite frequently. It'll give you an idea why we do some of the things we do. Specifications for our crew and equipment. Also a lot of the dos and don'ts for drivers."

She accepted the book and flipped through the pages. "Looks…interesting."

"You really don't have to be proficient with the technical stuff. You'll have an idea of what types of behavior NASCAR finds unacceptable. Cursing and fighting, to name two."

"That's understandable."

"Yes, some of it is just good common sense. I told

Michael yesterday that was one of the qualities I noticed about him right away. Not only is he intelligent, but he's got a good head on his shoulders, too—that's where the common sense comes in."

"He's a good boy. A good man," she amended.

"I told him he owes it all to you."

Her smile trembled. "Thank you. Sometimes I wondered if I would ever get it right."

"You did. He'll prove it to you, too."

"He doesn't have anything to prove."

Sam fleetingly wondered if he should tell her about Michael's speeding ticket, but decided against it. That was between her and Michael.

CHAPTER FIFTEEN

MICHAEL HEARD his mother's laughter through the door to their condo. The sound brought a smile to his lips. It was good to know she was having fun for the first time in a long while.

He felt a pang of guilt, wondering if he'd been the one to turn her so serious. Being a single mother had been hard, he knew, but she'd thrown herself into it wholeheartedly. But he'd never stopped to analyze what it had cost her.

When he opened the door, guilt fled, replaced by irritation when he saw the reason for her laughter. And a twinge of conscience at begrudging his mother the pleasure of a man's company. Boy, was he mixed up or what?

He tried to suppress his annoyance, instead greeting them a little too heartily. "Hey, Mom, Sam, you burning the midnight oil again?"

His mother's smile faded. "We were watching some old racing movies and documentaries. It's really fascinating the growth in the racing industry. And how long it's been around. Way back to the thirties."

"Men have probably been racing since the beginning

of time. Like, the cavemen were probably 'I bet my T-rex is faster than your old stegosaurus.'"

Sam chuckled. "No doubt. It's good to see you, Michael. What've you been up to now that Ron's cut back your training schedule through Christmas? Having five days a week to yourself must seem like a full vacation."

"Um, I've been spending a lot of time at the gym." He grabbed an orange from the fruit bowl and headed for his room. "See ya. I've got some stuff to do."

He breathed a sigh of relief when he reached his room. His mom would blow a gasket if she found out he'd been at defensive-driving school today. After the underage drinking and the fight, he'd be lucky if she'd trust him to race go-karts.

TESS FORGOT about Michael's behavior as she discussed the movies with Sam. "It's amazing, all the different types of personalities that go into NASCAR. I'd say it's a melting pot of styles if there ever was one."

"Absolutely. I think the chase for the cup has brought back the hunger, the edginess in the drivers."

Frowning, Tess said, "And that's supposed to reassure me?"

"You're getting the lingo and attitude of racing down so well, I forgot you were a mother in need of the sugar-coated version."

"And what's that?"

Sam's grin was wicked. "That these nice Sunday-school boys go out on the track and love their neighbors as themselves each week. The competition never gets tough and they're all self-effacing guys who wouldn't utter a naughty word."

"You forgot to mention that they walk on water."

"Darn near."

His smile warmed her, as did his leg so close to hers. No matter how hard she tried to keep space between them, they seemed to gravitate toward each other.

"Would they win like that?" she asked.

"Maybe. Maybe not. They *all* want to win."

"Human nature."

"You bet." He hesitated, then stood. "It's getting late. I better go. Oh, I almost forgot to ask you."

"Ask me what?"

"If you and Michael had plans for Christmas Day. Both my kids canceled on me. Looks like having their own lives gets complex at times. But I'm a whiz at cooking a turkey now and I thought you and Michael might join me for dinner?"

"Sam, you've been so sweet indoctrinating me in NASCAR lore the last couple weeks. The least I can do is cook the Christmas dinner. Would you join us here?"

"Whew." He wiped his brow. "I dodged that bullet. I would love it if you would handle the major cooking. I can pick up a pie and a nice bottle of wine."

"Sounds wonderful. But remember, you promised you'd let me take you antiquing this Saturday."

"I won't forget. I'll pick you up at eight."

"Nope. I'm driving this time. I'll pick you up at eight."

He grinned. "I love a woman who takes charge. See you Saturday."

She walked him to the door. He hesitated. The air was charged with undercurrents.

Tess hoped he would kiss her. Then hoped he wouldn't. But her body betrayed her, swaying close to him.

Tipping her chin with his finger, he said, "I had a great time today, Tess. I always have a great time with you. If you weren't Michael's mom, I'd ask you out in a heartbeat."

"If I weren't Michael's mom, I'd accept in a heartbeat," she murmured.

He dipped his head and kissed her on the lips. She could taste coffee and Sam.

"Ahem."

They separated to see Michael head for the kitchen. "I forgot a water bottle. See ya, Sam."

"Yes, see ya," Sam called. He kissed Tess on the cheek. "And I'll see you Saturday."

Tess closed the door after Sam left, smiling to herself.

"What's going on, Mom?"

Oh, Lord, she didn't want to have this conversation now.

"Nothing really. Sam's been teaching me the ins and outs of NASCAR."

"I bet." His sardonic tone grated on her nerves. Come to think of it, his changeable moods grated on her nerves, too. These days, it was impossible to know from one moment to the next if she'd be dealing with a rebellious teen or a centered, intelligent man.

"It's not like that. We enjoy each other's company,

so we spend time together. We've shared a couple harmless kisses and that's all."

"You're sure that's it?"

"Yes, I am."

"Okay. Well, I'm going to bed."

"Good night, dear."

"'Night."

Tess straightened the books and movies on the coffee table, wondering when she'd started having to answer to her teenage son about her choices.

Tess knew she could have attended Christmas Eve service by herself. She'd done it before when Michael had declined. But she was glad she hadn't this time.

Sam twined his fingers through hers as they walked the short distance from his truck to the community church.

"Michael refused to attend services tonight. Does there come a time when all children reject their parents' values, or is it just mine?"

"Depends on the kid. Stephanie mostly rebelled against her mom once she got in her teens, but I just figured it was female stuff."

"More and more, it seems Michael is becoming his father's son, taking on his value system, his characteristics. Funny, because his father has spent so little time with him."

"It's natural for boys to want to be like their dads."

Tess sighed. "I'd hoped I could encourage him to do things differently than his dad. To be responsible, to avoid risk. And I thought I'd succeeded, until this whole NASCAR thing."

"Hard to say. He's still pretty levelheaded. Maybe he's seeking his own identity and trying on different outlooks for size."

"He couldn't have tried on an accountant's outlook for a while?" Her lips twitched. "At least long enough so I could sleep at night."

"You're really losing sleep?"

She nodded. "Sometimes. I worry that he's going to run off to see the world like his father. Or get so immersed in racing, he forgets everything else. Then I'm convinced he'll never settle down and I'll never be a grandmother."

"You'd be an awfully young grandmother."

"I was an awfully young mother. Eighteen—Michael's age now, as a matter of fact."

"Is it the racing that bothers you most?"

"It scares me because I'm afraid it's something I can't share with him. Will he just leave me behind and create a NASCAR family of sorts? He already looks up to you like a father figure."

Sam stopped, grasping her other hand. He held her gaze. "Tess, Michael will never leave you behind, even if you don't know a caution flag from a restrictor plate."

"Fortunately, I do know the difference. Aren't you kind of…lonely…with your children living in another city?"

"I miss them like crazy sometimes, but it's also nice knowing I have freedom to live my life in the way that works for me. With small children, you do what's best for them, no questions asked. I can be a little selfish now and that's okay."

"I guess. I've felt selfish spending so much time with you. But then again, Ron implied I was only so much baggage."

Sam's tone was low when he said, "You're never baggage, Tess. You're incredibly important to Michael and his success. Never forget that."

"I'll try." They reached the church steps and entered the sanctuary.

The service started a few minutes after they sat down and Tess lost herself in the beauty and magic of a candlelight church service. Just as she lost herself in the steady warmth of Sam's hand as he clasped hers. And allowed herself to dream of being a part of a couple that lasted decades, not just a short while.

SAM KNOCKED at the McIntyres' door, whistling under his breath. He'd been hardly able to wait until one o'clock.

Tess opened the door, her hair brushed loosely around her shoulders, her deep-burgundy blouse setting off her delicate complexion.

He leaned down to kiss her cheek, inhaling her scent. A silky strand of her hair brushed his cheek. Closing his eyes, he rested his jaw against her head for just a moment.

He knew, in that moment, he was fighting a losing battle. He was falling for Tess, and falling hard.

She led him into the condo, offering a glass of wine. Suddenly nervous, he accepted. It seemed so right to spend this holiday with her. Could it have only been six months ago that they'd met? Two people wanting the best for Michael, but seeing it such different ways?

When she brought his wine, he drew her down onto the couch next to him. "I can't think of anywhere I'd rather be on Christmas Day. I only wish my children had come. I'd like you to meet them."

"I'd love to meet them, too."

"Can you believe it was only six months ago that we met?"

Tess smiled. "It seems like only yesterday I intended to toss you out of my house."

He grasped her hand. "No, you would never do anything as crass as to throw me out. You politely showed me the door, if I remember correctly."

"Lot of good it did." Her eyes sparkled.

"Persistence got me where I am today, figuratively and literally."

"You *are* persistent."

"And handsome."

"And handsome. Don't forget humble," she added.

"Of course. Humble."

He took her glass and placed it on the coffee table next to his. Tipping her chin with his finger, he touched his lips to hers, tasting wine and sweetness.

"And a good kisser." His voice was husky.

Her eyelids were half-closed. "Mmm. Definitely."

"And a total jerk."

Tess's eyelids sprang open.

Sam regretfully eased away from her.

They both turned to see Michael standing in the entryway, arms crossed, expression grim. "You know, you don't have to hit on my mom to keep me racing for you. She's…vulnerable."

Sam leaned back, resting his arm along the back of the couch, subtly claiming her. "That's a pretty insulting view of your mother, Michael. Tess is a smart, beautiful lady and I enjoy spending time with her, end of story. It has nothing to do with you or your racing for me. My team survived before I found you and I'm sure it'll survive if you decide to bail on us."

"My mom doesn't understand that guys like you aren't always what they seem."

"Guys like me?"

"You act like you're all concerned about her, about me. But you'll just run out on us when things get tough."

Tess raised her hand, palm outward. "Stop right there, Michael. Sam has done nothing but treat me with the utmost respect. And though I'm sure you want to believe your mother doesn't know the ways of the world, I'm not nearly as naive as you think."

"Oh, yeah? Then how come you never seriously dated after Dad left? Never remarried?"

"I was concentrating on my career and raising my son."

Her answer sounded carefully rehearsed. Sam wondered about the real story. There had to be a reason such a loving, giving woman had remained single for close to fifteen years.

Michael stepped close and knelt at her feet. "I was there when Dad left, remember? I was a little kid, but even I could see how deep the hurt went. Maybe you've been protecting yourself all these years. And maybe, in this case, protecting yourself is a good thing."

Tess cupped Michael's cheek with her hand. Her

voice was husky when she said, "I'm blessed to have a son who cares so much about me. You're spreading your wings to fly and that's as it should be. I think maybe it's time for me to test my wings, too."

Michael held Tess's gaze for a moment. Sam got a lump in his throat watching the wordless interchange.

Then Michael stood, his icy glare trained on Sam. "If you hurt her, you'll be sorry."

In that moment, Sam realized clearly that Michael McIntyre had crossed the line from childhood to adulthood and would never look back.

"I promise not to hurt her." He held Michael's gaze, though he was aware it was a promise no human being could keep. Even the very best relationships had growing pains. But, despite Michael's flashes of maturity, Sam didn't think he was ready to hear that hard truth of adulthood.

CHAPTER SIXTEEN

TESS'S HEART CONTRACTED at the thought of her son defending her honor, as if she were some fragile, wounded creature. Was that how he saw her? All while she'd convinced herself she was a strong, independent woman?

She felt as if her blinders had fallen away. Her carefully constructed world, full of soothing routine and safety from disruptions had convinced him she couldn't handle the real world. That she'd created her own fantasy place to avoid the harsh realities of life.

Her pulse pounded as she contemplated something so horrific it made her sweat. What if he was right?

Had she thrown away possibly the best years of her life by being afraid? Was it the real reason she'd devoted herself to the noble cause of single motherhood and putting her child first?

But she had to tell Michael something. "Sam and I aren't serious, Michael. We're friends first and foremost."

She glanced at Sam and swallowed hard. He meant more to her than she was ready to face. "We're testing the romantic waters, taking things slowly. We haven't even really dated."

Sam laughed. "And here I thought all those afternoons spent filling food boxes were dates." He clutched his chest. "You wound me."

His teasing eased the tenseness in the room.

She bumped him with her shoulder. "Not even close, buddy. If we're dating, you'll know it. I want champagne and roses and declarations of love."

Michael made a noise low in his throat that might have indicated disgust. Or signaled impending illness.

"I'll be in my room checking my e-mail. Let me know when dinner's ready." He turned and left the room.

Tess raised an eyebrow. "I guess his protectiveness has a time limit."

"Or a gag response. We could have really had some fun with him and told him we were planning on procreating."

"Please, no, then he'd be out buying a shotgun. One shotgun wedding in a lifetime is enough."

"Really? You had a shotgun wedding?"

She shrugged. "Not in the literal sense. The intent was the same, though."

Sam grasped her chin with his hand. "Hey, look at me. How come you act as if you're ashamed?"

"It wasn't the best way to get married. And I always thought Royce felt as if I'd trapped him."

"It takes two to tango. Although Candace and I had a remarkably similar situation, I never felt trapped. Just felt it was a natural consequence to unprotected sex. Of course, I was head over heels in love at the time, too."

"Really? Men can go head over heels?"

"You bet. We just don't show it the same way as women."

"So what are the signs?"

He seemed to consider her question. "Phoning every day, introducing a woman to our friends, agreeing to going places we don't really want to go, doing things we don't really want to do."

"Wow, that's really definitive. That describes casual dating to me."

"Ah, the old Mars-Venus thing. Probably with guys it's the stuff women *don't* see. Like thinking of her all the time, even in the middle of a close Cup race, wanting to be with her more than guy friends, and not just because of sex. Stuff like that."

Tess felt a twinge of jealousy. "Has this happened to you often?"

"Nope. With my ex, it was the old cliché. We simply grew apart. I've dated, but nothing serious." He wiped his brow in mock relief. "Whew."

Taking his lead, she said, "Enough of the serious contemplation. It's Christmas Day and celebration is in order. I'll get supper on the table and we feast."

"I hope you didn't show me up in the turkey-cooking department." He sniffed the air. "Though I don't smell the aroma of my nemesis."

"No, I cooked a ham instead. Candied sweet potatoes. Tamales…"

"Tamales?"

"A tradition I've picked up from friends in Phoenix. I haven't mastered the art of making them myself, though I've tried. A friend shipped a batch to me in dry ice."

"Ah. I look forward to trying them. I'm always up for new experiences."

She eyed him thoughtfully. "So was my ex-husband. Why is it I'm always attracted to risk takers?"

He slid his arm around her waist. "So you admit you're attracted to me?"

"I figured you might have gotten that impression already. I don't generally kiss men I find unattractive."

"Aha! So you're attracted to me *and* think I'm attractive. Always a good sign."

She smacked him playfully on the shoulder. "As if you need me to feed your ego."

"No, my ego is quite healthy already. But a snack now and then doesn't hurt. Now, tell me what you need me to help with in the kitchen. I didn't intend to be a total slacker."

They shared stories of Christmases past and family traditions as they transferred food from the oven to the table Tess had already set.

Sam stopped in his tracks, holding the platter with the ham.

"Wow," he breathed. "This is really...nice."

Tess warmed at his praise. "I know you've probably eaten at some elegant tables and there's no way I can compete with that. So I went for the homey Christmas theme."

Sam thought Tess must have an overly glamorous view of his life. He was much more impressed by heart and sincerity.

"Oh, you succeeded. And managed both homey Christmas and elegant." He placed the platter on the trivet and went to wrap his arms around her. "Thank you, Tess, for making this holiday special."

"Thank you for making mine." And she glanced toward the ceiling, an impish light in her eyes. "Mistletoe."

He pulled her close and kissed her.

She twined her arms around his neck, inviting him to deepen the kiss. He murmured her name, parting her lips to explore all that was Tess.

"Ahem. This is really getting old. I'd tell you two to get a room, but that is so not going to happen on my watch. I'm more of the unhand-her-you-wretch school."

Sam reluctantly let Tess go. "You know, your timing sucks, kid."

Michael's eyes narrowed. "First, I'm not a kid. And second, I think my timing is pretty darn good. Looks like yours is off, old man."

Them's fighting words.

And it appeared as if that was exactly what Michael had intended.

Sam took a deep breath and chose to find the humor in the situation. Chuckling, he said, "No one's ever called me 'old man' before. And I thought 'mister' made me feel old."

Michael nodded, apparently satisfied that he'd taken Sam down a notch. Probably figuring if Sam's ego were deflated, he wouldn't pursue Tess. Little did he know, Sam's ego was healthy enough to withstand the barbs.

"Let's eat before the food cools," Tess said, her smile forced.

"Yes. Let's."

He sat where Tess indicated and bowed his head as

she led them in grace. He was distinctly aware of Michael's hot glare the whole time.

Sam was tempted to tattle, but decided to be adult about it.

He was glad he'd used restraint, because the meal conversation settled into a pleasant give and take, full of laughter and affection.

When supper was finished and he and Michael had helped clear the table and load the dishwasher, they went into the great room for pumpkin pie and coffee.

A fire snapped and crackled in the fireplace. Sam sighed. "Wonderful dinner, Tess. Thank you."

"You're quite welcome." Tess cleared the plates. When she returned from the kitchen, she chose a wrapped package from under the tree. "This is a little something from Michael and me."

Sam carefully removed the wrapping paper.

Tess chuckled. "I would have had you pegged for a rip-and-tear kind of guy."

He glanced up and caught her eye. "Unwrapping a gift is like lots of life's endeavors—better savored slowly and with care."

Tess's cheeks grew pink.

Michael muttered, "Just open it already."

Sam's throat got all scratchy when he opened the box and pushed back the tissue paper. It was a small throw pillow with one of his cars embroidered on the front. At the top, it read, Kincaid Racing and along the bottom edge, it read Sam in elegant script.

Clearing his throat, he asked, "Did you make it?"

"Yes."

"I'll treasure it always."

Michael made a rude noise, but Sam ignored him as he held Tess's gaze. Then he remembered something.

He stood, went to the coat tree and fished two small packages out of his coat pockets. He handed one to Michael and one to Tess.

Michael tore into his package with all the glee of a child, his pique temporarily forgotten. He removed a platinum key chain, No. 463. "Cool."

"That's going to be your number in the NASCAR Busch Series."

"All right. Thanks, man."

He turned to Tess as she removed the wrapping paper from her gift. Opening the box, her eyes widened. She withdrew the delicate charm bracelet. "It's beautiful," she breathed. "The significance of the charms?"

Sam had chosen three charms with care. "The race car was custom molded based on a picture I gave the jeweler—Michael's car next year."

"The 463 is for his number," she noted. "And the heart?"

Her eyes lit. Appreciation? Hope? Christmas spirit?

His voice was husky when he said, "The heart represents your heart, which will be with Michael every time he races."

"Thank you. It's very special."

He wondered if it would have been more special if he'd told her it represented his heart, which she'd stolen from the moment he'd met her. But that would have been overstating his growing interest in her.

Wouldn't it?

TESS MISSED Sam. She hadn't talked to him in four days and it was killing her. Funny, she didn't seem to mind the fact that Michael was gone from early morning to well after dark. She couldn't even seem to get too distracted by thoughts of what trouble he might be getting into.

No, she was more distracted by thoughts of what Sam might be doing. Usually she talked to him every couple days. But the food bank was inundated with volunteers doing their once-a-year feel-good work, so they'd graciously given the regulars the week between Christmas and New Year off.

Her bracelet jangled at her wrist as she reached for her address book. The platinum charms sparkled and moved, an ever-changing tribute to Kincaid Racing. And her heart.

Tess decided she'd been passive too long. She needed to hear Sam's voice. Dialing his cell, she held her breath until he answered.

"Hi, Sam, it's Tess. I just wanted to thank you again for my bracelet."

Sam groaned. "I meant to call you. My kids were able to meet me in Chicago for a few brief days. I just got back to Charlotte."

"How nice that you were able to spend some time with them after all."

"Yes, it was great."

I'd like to meet them. No way could she say that. It would sound as if she had expectations.

"I'm glad. Apparently Ron indicated a car is being built for Michael. He's pretty excited."

"Yep. February will be here before we know it. I'm

glad you called, by the way. Some friends of mine are having a New Year's Eve party and I wondered if you'd go with me. A real date."

Tess was glad Michael wasn't home, because she grinned from ear to ear. "I'd love to. It sounds fun."

"Remember, it's one of the signs a guy is falling for a woman."

"What is?"

"That I'm taking you to meet my friends."

"Oh." Wow. It was what she'd wanted, but now she had a hard time taking it all in.

"Are you okay with that? I'm not moving too fast?"

"I think your timing is perfect. I'd love to meet your friends."

His voice was husky when he said, "Good, because I really want to ring in the New Year with you, Tess."

Tess took a deep breath. "I feel the same."

"See you at eight Tuesday? It's black-tie."

MICHAEL SUPPRESSED a pang of guilt as he let himself into the condo. He hadn't been home much lately, hadn't spent much time with his mom. And here he was home long enough to shower, shave and meet some of the guys for New Year's Eve.

"Mom, I'm home," he called.

The lights were on and it appeared she was home.

He tapped on her bedroom door. No answer. Now he was starting to get worried. What if she'd gotten sick and nobody had been here to help?

Pushing open her door, he glanced inside. That's

when he heard her shower running. And singing. Since when did Mom sing in the shower?

Michael shrugged, closing her bedroom door. What did he care, as long as she wasn't nagging him about never being home? His conscience reminded him that his mother didn't nag.

He went to his own room, and emerged a half hour later, showered, shaved and dressed in jeans and a casual shirt. Shooting pool didn't require a lot of attention to wardrobe detail. Glancing at his reflection in the mirror, he hoped he might meet some hot girls, though.

Glancing at his watch, Michael realized he had some time to kill before meeting the guys. He grabbed a snack and used the remote to flick on the TV.

It seemed like only a few minutes later when the doorbell rang.

Opening the door, he was surprised to find Sam standing on the other side, dressed in a tuxedo, no less. He held a single red rose.

"Hey, Sam, what're you doing here?"

"I'm here to pick up Tess. We're going to a New Year's Eve party."

Michael muttered something vague and opened the door wide to allow Sam in—though he wanted to slam the door in the guy's face. He'd liked Sam, until he'd started hitting on his mom.

"I'll tell her you're here," he said, his tone grudging. He tapped on her door. "Mom, Sam's here."

"I'll be right there," she called.

Michael went and sat down on the couch. What kind of small talk did you make under these circumstance?

What are your intentions toward my mother?

No, that sounded way too weird. Instead, he opted for "So, is this, like, a date?"

"Yes, it is. I want you to know I think your mom is a pretty special lady."

"Yeah, she is. New Year strikes at midnight. You should have her back here by twelve-thirty, right?"

Sam grinned and shrugged.

Tess's bedroom door opened and Michael caught a whiff of the perfume she only wore for special occasions. Turning, he felt his jaw drop open.

Sam whistled, low and appreciative. "Tess, you look gorgeous."

His mother stepped into the room and pirouetted, the skirt to her navy-blue silk gown billowing around her. When she stopped, he noticed her cheeks were pink, her eyes sparkled, matching the diamonds at her throat. She still wore the charm bracelet, though.

"You look pretty handsome yourself, Sam."

Standing, Sam seemed to have eyes only for Tess. He extended the rose. "For you."

"No champagne?" Her laugh was throaty and seductive. Mothers were *not* supposed to laugh that way. And then Michael realized what a large expanse of skin the dress bared. His mother was showing cleavage!

Horror washed over him. *Lots* of cleavage.

Michael knew he could have gone to his grave without seeing that. And with his mother standing next to Sam, gazing up into his eyes, they looked almost like a couple of teens on prom night.

Michael swallowed hard. Everyone knew what happened on prom night.

He stepped forward. "Hey, guys, I'd love to go to a New Year's Eve party. How about if I join you?"

His mother and Sam replied in unison, "No."

That was it. No "Sorry you're going to have a crummy New Year's all by yourself." No "Sorry we're being selfish and want to rip each other's clothes off the minute we leave."

They simply headed for the door.

Finally, Tess turned and said, "Oh, Michael?"

"Yes?" His voice rose hopefully.

"Don't wait up."

CHAPTER SEVENTEEN

SAM COULDN'T SEEM to get enough of Tess; her laughter, the softness of her skin, the promise in her eyes. The way she was able to converse with anyone at the party and set people instantly at ease.

She even danced superbly, helping him feel as if he were more than a merely competent dancer.

Sam pulled her close and murmured in her ear, "What do you think of the party?"

She rested her head against his shoulder for a moment. "It's wonderful. The music, the food, all very elegant. I've seen a few faces I recognize from the track, along with a few from the society pages."

"You wanted champagne and roses and I delivered. Do I get bonus points for caviar?"

Wrinkling her nose, she said, "Definitely not. You might, however, earn extra credit when you kiss me at midnight."

"How about if I kiss you now?"

"No extra points." She tilted her head. "But you wouldn't be penalized, either."

"In that case…" He placed a kiss on the corner of her mouth.

"Mmm." Her throaty response sent awareness humming through him.

He kissed her cheek, her jaw. Nipped at her earlobe.

"Oh, that is so not nice," she murmured.

"No?" He nibbled again and felt her shiver.

"No more. If you keep that up, I'll never make it till our midnight kiss. And I really want to properly welcome the New Year with you, Sam."

He leaned back so he could see her face. Her eyes were serious. "It's that important?"

"I feel like I've started a whole new life since I've come to Charlotte. I want to embrace the New Year and all the good things in store. And I want to open myself up to new experiences, new blessings." She lowered her eyes, as if suddenly shy. "I hope one of them will be you."

At another time, another place, such a declaration might have scared him silly. But here, tonight, with Tess, it seemed to embody the hope for a new year, a brilliant new relationship.

"I hope so, too."

They danced and danced, chatted with friends and snagged a glass of champagne several hours later as midnight approached.

Together, in their own little world, they counted down to the New Year. "Ten, nine, eight…"

Sam ignored the jostles as everyone flooded the dance floor. He only had eyes for his beautiful Tess.

"…seven, six, five, four…"

He cupped her face with his hand, rubbing his thumb along her jaw.

"...three, two, one. Happy New Year!"

He bent his head to kiss her. It went on and on, well into the New Year, as his senses swam and he lost his heart to Tess McIntyre.

Sam so wanted to invite her back to his place for an evening of lovemaking, but for some reason it just didn't seem right. Maybe because Tess was a special, classy lady. Or maybe because he didn't want to jinx what they had by rushing her. Or maybe because he suspected Michael would be waiting up for her return.

When Sam saw her to her door at nearly 2:00 a.m., he found his suspicions were correct. The door opened immediately and Michael glowered while Sam quickly kissed Tess good-night.

But even that didn't dampen Sam's spirits. Because he'd seen the promise in Tess's eyes. There would be many more evenings to come. Evenings where her son wasn't playing chaperone.

Sam whistled a tune as he walked to his car. The New Year promised to be the best ever.

TESS SORTED THROUGH the forwarded mail she'd picked up at the post office. Phoenix seemed like a lifetime ago.

A thick manila envelope was on top of the stack, almost as if demanding attention. The return address was Stanford.

Slicing the envelope with an opener, she pulled out the sheaf of papers. She ran her index finger over the letterhead, enjoying the substantial feel of academia at its finest.

She was almost afraid to read the letter. It said how

much they hoped Michael would reapply for his scholarship. The paperwork was enclosed.

Tess closed her eyes, revisiting her dream of Michael at Stanford. But the dream wasn't nearly as clear as it had been six months ago. Because it involved an old life that didn't fit so well anymore.

When Tess opened the front door, she was reminded of one of the major reasons her old life wasn't a good fit.

"Sam," she murmured and walked into his arms.

"You look distracted. You haven't forgotten our date, have you?" he teased, pulling her close for a kiss.

"No, as if I could." She drew him into the condo and closed the door.

"Then why the frown?"

"We received a letter from Stanford today. They're still very eager to have Michael attend there. I can't help but wonder if I've let Michael down. If he'll resent me one day for not forcing him to do the prudent thing."

"Just the opposite, Tess. I was forced into the family construction business after high-school graduation and I've resented it ever since. The family business was considered stable, safe. Did I ever tell you I wanted to be a pro baseball player? But that usually meant four years of college ball, then the minors. My folks couldn't understand wasting all that time, when I had a sure deal at home. When I found out Candace was pregnant, I caved." He shook his head, his voice low. "I've always wondered if I could have made it."

"You never felt Candace trapped you?"

"No, she would have loved me no matter what. I

guess it was my own sense of responsibility that helped make the decision. The concept of becoming a parent was enough adventure. I figured I didn't need any more."

"Don't you suppose your parents might have been right, Sam? Things seemed to turn out pretty well for you."

"But I'll always wonder if maybe I might have had it all. Give Michael his dreams, Tess, allow him to fail or succeed on his own merits. Then he won't always wonder what might have been."

"I guess I'm feeling a little guilty. I haven't been focused on Michael much lately. And I'm afraid I've just turned him loose because I'm distracted...with our relationship."

He drew her close. "You've been a fabulous mother to Michael. You've given him the room to grow because that's what's right for him, not because you and I got involved."

"I guess you're right." But she couldn't help feeling a little selfish for pursuing her own happiness when Michael was at such a critical point in his life.

She sighed. "It's all so complex."

THE NEXT FEW WEEKS WENT by in a blur. And yet, time couldn't seem to move fast enough for Sam. He'd watched Michael train, watched him grow and mature. The guy was ready for the challenge of NASCAR.

As for Tess, their relationship grew and matured, too. She was frequently on his mind when he awoke in the morning and was his last thought at night. He'd never really expected a second chance at love and was a little in awe of the gift.

Neither of them spoke of their six-month contract.

Sam had arranged to meet Tess and Michael at the track one Thursday, eager to have them share in his excitement.

"What's this all about?" Tess asked.

"Yeah, why all the secrecy?" Michael seemed taller, broader than when he'd come to Charlotte. The weight training and cardiovascular workouts were effective.

"I've got something to show you over here." He led them to a bay. Grasping the edge of the car cover, he waited expectantly. Too bad he hadn't arranged a drumroll.

"Sam, the suspense is killing me. Show us." Tess's eyes sparkled with enjoyment. She reminded him of a kid on Christmas Day. How had he ever thought her to be rigid and tedious?

With a flourish, Sam withdrew the cover. The No. 463 car gleamed beneath the fluorescent lighting, silver accents on navy blue.

"It's beautiful," Tess breathed. In that moment, he knew racing had gotten under her skin, despite her protests to the contrary. She moved closer, reaching out as if to touch the hood. She stopped short. "May I?"

"You bet. You, too, Michael. This is your ride for the season."

Michael let out a low whistle as he walked around the car. "Wow."

"Yeah, wow," Sam said. "Get in and turn it over."

Michael slid in through the window as if he'd been

doing it all his life. His wide smile told Sam the boy had finally come home.

Sam stepped closer to Tess, sliding his arm around her waist. "Any doubt that's exactly where he belongs?"

"It certainly appears so."

"It's just the beginning. He'll take this car and a backup to every race. Then there will be practice cars, too."

It was Tess's turn to let out a low whistle. "The motors alone are about eighty thousand dollars apiece, aren't they?"

"Yes. You've been doing your homework. It's an expensive sport. But worth every penny, in my opinion."

The raw need revealed in Michael's expression as he started the engine told Sam everything he wanted to know. Michael McIntyre was born to race. As if there had ever been any doubt.

CHAPTER EIGHTEEN

TESS WAS a nervous wreck, waiting for the race to start. This was Daytona, the ultimate in racing. And Michael's first time racing with the big boys.

And, like any mother, she was worried her son might get bullied on the playground. A concern that outweighed her questions about returning to Phoenix. Like how much longer she could stay in Charlotte if Sam didn't bring up their original six-month deadline. And what it would mean to their relationship when she did leave.

Sam grasped her hand. "Relax, it'll be fine."

"Maybe we should have sat on top of the hauler. That way I'd be closer if something hap—"

"Nothing's going to happen. Michael's been training hard for this day. He's got a top-notch car, crew and chief. He'll be fine. Remember how well protected he is in the cockpit?"

She nodded. "So well protected, it made me a little claustrophobic when I sat in the car." Hesitating, she said, "You really think those evasive-action exercises helped?"

"Absolutely. He's familiar with this car now, too."

"That's a good thing. As long as he doesn't get overconfident."

"For his first NASCAR Busch Series race, I guarantee you he won't get overconfident. As a matter of fact, if he's like most drivers in their first NASCAR race, he's probably puking right now."

Tess started to rise. "I better go check—"

Sam grasped her arm and eased her back into her seat. "No, you won't. The last thing he needs is his mama checking on him. You'd make him the laughing-stock of the pit area."

Crossing her arms over her chest, Tess said, "Well, they need to be more progressive in their thinking. Who says a man can't be both a tough driver and have a soft spot for his mama?"

His expression was thoughtful. "That's definitely an angle the marketing people might want to exploit. It's worked well for other young drivers."

"Aha! I'm right."

He grinned. "I can't tell you that, or you'll never let me hear the end of it."

"But there might be fringe benefits." She was thinking of a home-cooked meal.

His eyes widened. "I like the sound of that."

Sam obviously had other ideas. The thought alternately thrilled and dismayed her. They hadn't been intimate in deference to Michael's tender emotions about his mother's honor. Or at least that was the excuse she'd given Sam. Truth was, she found Sam sexy as hell, but the thought of taking their relationship to the next level scared her. The last time she'd loved a man this completely, he'd left her. And, though she told herself the situations were completely different, she feared Sam would grow bored and leave. He was, after all, a risk taker like her ex.

"Drivers, start your engines," came through the speakers, pulling Tess out of her reverie.

She held her breath as the green flag dropped. The car in the pole position took the lead, the other cars jockeying for a spot right behind it.

She cheered herself hoarse as Michael found his line and settled into sixth place. Glancing at Sam, she asked, "It's a good start, isn't it?"

"Damn good start for his first big race."

"Now if he can just make a good pit stop."

"You bet."

"He was very nervous about that. He told me that he practiced and practiced with Ron and thought he had it down. But with his adrenaline flowing, all the confusion down there and forty-two other drivers looking for their team flags, he might miss it completely."

"He'll do fine. It's the first race of the season and everyone's getting used to their cars. Some have new crews, new teams entirely. He won't be the only one settling in."

"Kind of like the first day of school."

"Exactly."

"He was so excited. And petrified. Though he'd probably be upset that I told you that."

"I'm not surprised. I'd worry if he wasn't."

Tess watched the No. 463 car, in awe that her little boy was driving that machine. And wondering where all the time had gone. "It seems like only yesterday I was teaching him to ride a two-wheeler."

"They grow up fast. But just think of the fun you'll have with grandkids."

"Bite your tongue—he's only eighteen." Her eyes grew misty at the thought. "I would like grandkids to spoil someday in the distant future."

"My son and daughter aren't in any hurry to get married and settle down, thank goodness."

"Speaking of children, I've been thinking of something. There are so many worthy charities supported by NASCAR teams and the NASCAR Foundation—there has to be something more suited to my strengths and interests."

"Ah, I wondered how long it would be before you got bored assembling food boxes."

"Don't get me wrong, I'll still volunteer there. But my heart is more in the area of education and literacy. Surely there has to be something else I can do?"

"I'll look into it. I can probably have a couple names and numbers for you on Monday, if that's soon enough?"

"That would be great. There is such a need and I feel like I might be a good fit."

The announcer's excited voice cut into their conversation, reminding them why they were there. "That had to hurt. Looks like the No. 79 car got loose in the turn and took the No. 53 car with him. Newcomer Michael McIntyre managed to get around the whole mess."

Tess released a breath. "He's okay. He did well. The evasive-action exercises worked."

"Yep, bumper cars. Part of the exercise is for the driver to grow accustomed to what it feels like to get hit. The anticipation is usually worse than the actual hit."

Most of the drivers pulled into the pits for the yellow caution flag. Michael pulled in, too. He found his stall, but overshot by a few feet.

"Not bad. The timing doesn't always have to be perfect on a yellow."

The crew pushed the vehicle back a few feet and went to work.

Sam put on his headphones, listening intently.

Tess put on the pair he'd supplied to her.

Hearing Michael's voice, calm, cool and collected, she was so proud. He'd tackled every challenge put in front of him to get here tonight.

The pit stop was done before she knew it. Michael resumed his place in line, now fourth. The incident had moved him ahead two spots.

"Kind of like a batter being walked to bring in a run, but there's still skill involved," Sam commented.

Tilting her head, Tess said, "Yes, you're right. I guess I'm going to have to start paying more attention to baseball, too."

Sam chuckled. "Only if you want to. Michael is doing really well. If he can hold off the cars behind and make a late bid for the front, he's got a shot at the lead."

"Who'd have thought the little boy who was afraid of the log-jam ride at the theme park would turn out to be a top stock-car driver?"

"He's come a long way, all right, just in the time I've known him. Of course I take all the credit." Sam grinned.

"Just like a man. And, of course, my participation in sixteen hours of labor and raising him for eighteen years was unimportant."

Wrapping his arm around her, Sam squeezed her shoulder. "No way. You have the most important job of all, hands down."

"That's twice tonight you've admitted I'm right. This is getting a little scary."

"What, that I can admit I'm wrong?"

"You've got to remember, I work with attorneys. I don't think I can recall a single one admitting to being wrong."

"Occupational hazard, I guess."

"Yes, that and the proliferation of attorney jokes. And everyone I meet at a party wants free legal advice. Attorney, paralegal, they're usually not picky who dispenses it."

"Do you miss it?"

"Not nearly as much as I thought I would."

"Do I sense a career change coming on?"

Tess was amazed that Sam managed to sense what she was thinking almost as soon as she did. It was uncanny. "I've been doing some reevaluating. Now that Michael's going to be on his own pretty soon, I'm thinking of making a change. I've always wanted to be an elementary-school teacher."

"So why'd you become a paralegal?"

"Two reasons. One, the paralegal degree took three years as opposed to four for a teaching degree. Two, I could make a good, consistent living without having to count on child support."

"Your ex didn't pay?"

"He did, but he had stretches between jobs. Since he worked outside the United States, child support got tricky. It was easier if I didn't count on it. Most went for Michael's tuition."

There was another wreck toward the back of the pack. It was minor, but resulted in another caution flag.

Sam touched her arm. "You know, Tess, you mentioned you were afraid Michael's father thought you'd trapped him."

"Yes."

He turned her face towards his. "I think he should have felt like the luckiest guy alive to have you."

Tess's eyes misted. "What a beautiful thing to say."

"It's the absolute truth."

Tess tipped her head and kissed him. The noisy melody of the track faded. She knew, somewhere in the back of her mind, that this was a momentous evening for her son. She also knew it was a momentous evening for her. She'd fallen just a little in love with Sam Kincaid. And somehow she'd get past the fear that he might leave.

MICHAEL LEVERED himself out the window.

Ron clapped him on the back. "Third place. Impressive, Michael."

Michael's heart swelled with pride. Ron wasn't a demonstrative man at best. That made his words of praise mean all the more.

"Looks like a sportscaster from one of the local stations is headed this way. You're on your way, kid."

Michael swallowed hard. This was the part of the job he felt least prepared for.

The newscaster introduced himself and told Michael it would be a live feed. They just needed a sound bite from the up-and-coming driver taking the NASCAR Busch Series by storm.

Michael smiled, bemused. They were laying it on a little thick, but heck, he'd play along. The short interview was over before he knew it. And he'd managed not to say anything too stupid.

Then he spotted his mom as she made her way through the crowd. He enfolded her in a big hug. "What'd you think, Mom?"

Did I do good? He felt like a kindergartner displaying a prized finger painting.

Her smile was as broad as if he'd graduated from Stanford. "I'm so proud of you."

"I'm kind of proud of myself."

Sam walked up and extended his hand. "Good job, son."

Michael's exultation dimmed. He wasn't Sam's son and he didn't want the guy getting any ideas that he needed a stepfather this late in the game. He'd always envisioned his mom living out her old age in their house in Phoenix—loving, supportive and always available.

Selfish? Yes, he supposed it was. But no matter how hard he tried to accept her relationship with Sam, he couldn't help feeling Sam was taking advantage of her. How could he pretend to support a relationship he suspected would only hurt her in the end?

CHAPTER NINETEEN

"I'LL BE in the NASCAR NEXTEL Cup Series by next year. Who knows, I might even be voted rookie of the year this year. That would be totally cool."

Tess opened her mouth to tell Michael not to count his chickens before they hatched, but she refrained. She'd been the voice of caution for too long. And apparently, she'd been absolutely wrong.

"You certainly are doing well, honey," she said, patting his arm.

"Yes, you are." Sam wasn't as pleased as he should have been, considering Michael's phenomenal rise in the ranks. Maybe he was as uneasy as she was. Or maybe he had other things on his mind, like second-guessing their relationship.

She had no idea where that idea came from. Sam had given her no indication whatsoever that he was unhappy with her. But then again, she'd never seen the signs with Royce, either.

It seemed that the more smoothly their relationship went, the more she had thoughts like these. Her stuff, left over from the wreckage of her marriage, she supposed. Shaking her head, Tess forced the insecurities away.

"Hey, another third place week before last, then first place this week. I was born to win," Michael crowed.

Tess managed to stay silent, but it took tremendous effort. His bragging was out of character and not very endearing. Hopefully, he'd get over himself.

Michael picked up a manila envelope on the side table, where it had gathered dust. "What was this stuff from Stanford about?"

"It's the paperwork to reapply for your scholarship. You can't blame them for being persistent."

He tossed the envelope down. "Yeah, well, I'm going to be too busy nailing the Busch Series and after that, The Cup."

She glanced at Sam and rolled her eyes.

He said, "Those are some pretty big predictions, Michael. Of course, that's the kind of thing we're hoping for. But, truth be told, it doesn't happen that way for many guys so early on. There's a learning curve involved."

Michael playfully punched Sam's shoulder. "Yeah, but haven't you heard, I'm the new phenom. I run faster than a speeding locomotive, catch bullets in my teeth, drive with both arms tied behind my back…"

"Hold on there, son. Don't get too big of an ego or somebody'll figure you need to be knocked down a notch."

"Let them try. I'm ready." Michael boxed the air for a moment before jogging out of the room.

"I'm worried about him," Tess said.

"And that's something new?"

"No, I guess not. I'm afraid he's overconfident."

Sam stepped close and wrapped his arms around her waist, nuzzling her neck from behind. "I have to admit, I'm afraid of the same thing, sweetheart. We can advise him, but if he doesn't listen there's not a whole lot we can do."

She sighed, reveling in the safety of his arms while steadfastly keeping her emotional baggage at bay.

"I never thought I'd be afraid of success for my son. Have we created an overconfident monster?"

"You've raised him well. I'm willing to bet he's solid as a rock beneath all that bragging."

"I sure hope so. Lately, I've begun to wonder if I know him at all."

"He'll settle in." He hesitated. "And if he doesn't, life has a way of teaching us to be humble."

"True. I just hope he doesn't have to learn his lessons the hard way."

"No parent does."

"Your other driver seems to be doing well, too."

"Yes, but not as well as Michael. They make good teammates. Michael's youth balances Vance's seasoning. Michael needs a little more attention, while Vance seems to thrive on as little interference from me as possible."

"I never realized so much psychology went into owning a racing team."

"It's like parenting. You adjust to the different personalities of your children."

Tess turned in his arms so she faced him. "Sam Kincaid, you are a very wise man. Sexy, too."

"How do you always know how to say the right

thing? Just when I thought you'd forgotten making love might be in our future." He bent his head and trailed kisses along her neck.

She groaned in frustration. "I want that, too. Soon."

He nipped her bottom lip. "How soon?"

"When I think Michael can handle it."

"Don't you mean when you can stand up to your son and tell him you deserve a life of your own?"

"That might not be the best approach." She hesitated. "Sam, I have a confession to make."

"Sounds serious."

"I haven't been completely honest with you."

"Oh?" His face went expressionless.

"The waiting hasn't all been because of Michael. Part of it's me."

Sam brushed a lock of hair off her forehead. "So what's it all about?" His voice was so patient, so kind, she wanted to cry. How could she doubt this man?

"Our relationship is so good sometimes it scares me." She glanced away, unable to meet his eyes, afraid of what she might see there.

"Let me get this straight. You don't want to make love because we get along too well?"

Nodding, she said, "In a way. When things are going really well, I get this weird thought that you're going to eventually get bored and leave. So I hold back."

"Have I ever given you that impression?"

"That's just it. You haven't. I...I guess it's leftover stuff from my marriage to Royce."

His gaze was warm, concerned. "Then we'll wait until you're ready. I have no intention of going anywhere."

"Thanks, Sam. It means a lot…I'm sorry for—"

He placed his finger over her lips. "Shh. That's not something you need to apologize for. When our relationship moves forward, it will be because both of us are one hundred percent ready. No regrets, no what-ifs."

Tess blinked back tears.

I love you, Sam.

She couldn't voice the words. It was too soon. And too many what-ifs still distracted her. But someday, she hoped to be able to tell him what was in her heart.

SAM STOOD in his office and stared out the picture window. He absently tossed the baseball from one hand to the other.

A tap sounded at his door.

"Come in."

Michael strolled in. "Hey, Ron said you wanted to see me."

"Sit." Sam motioned to the chair opposite his desk. "I've been hearing some unsettling rumors."

Michael's eyes widened. A guilty flush crept up his neck. "Rumors?"

"You've been bringing girls to the motor home when it's parked in Charlotte."

"Oh, come on, Sam. I share a condo with my mom. What am I supposed to do?"

"Abstain?" The thought was out before he could consider his audience.

Michael's disbelieving laugh confirmed his audacity. "Yeah, right. I've got fans now."

"Look, kid, you'll always have women throwing

themselves at you. Since your father isn't here, I'll give you the talk I think he probably would. Women should be treated with respect. Quick, meaningless sex is not going to make you happy."

The guy had the nerve to smirk. Sam could almost see the wheels turning in his near genius head, figuring Sam was too old at forty-five to feel passionately about a woman. If only Michael knew.

Sam shook his head, trying desperately to get Tess from his mind. How much he cared for her, how much he wanted to make love with her.

"Let me put it another way. Quick, meaningless sex could kill you."

"I know about using protection."

"Good. Do you use it every single time?"

Michael couldn't meet his eyes. "Come on, man. This is none of your business."

Sam took a deep breath, mentally cursing himself for thinking it was a good idea to hire an eighteen-year-old. But then he never would have met Tess if he hadn't hired Michael.

"Did you note the morals clause in your contract?" he asked, his voice deceptively calm.

"Yeah, I remember reading something about that."

"That means your extracurricular activities *are* my business. Not to mention the fact that it would disappoint your mother greatly if those rumors got back to her."

Michael straightened. "You're not going to tell my mom, are you?"

"If you continue the way you are, I will. I'll also

exercise my right to invoke the morals clause. This recklessness needs to stop. First it was the fighting and underage drinking. Now it's dangerous behavior of another kind. You're testing your limits—that's only natural. Now I'm defining those limits for you. No more romantic interludes at the track, in the motor home, the hauler, the garage or the condo. Better get your head straight and concentrate on your future. A future thousands of men would love to have."

"Hey, man, I'm winning. What more do you want?"

"I want to see a mature man with a good head on his shoulders. One who intends to be the best driver, the best *man,* he can possibly be through hard work and dedication."

"Sure. Whatever."

Sam's stomach churned. What if Tess had been right all along and fame ended up destroying Michael's future?

Sam had a difficult decision to make. And Michael's behavior indicated he'd better make it soon.

TESS HUMMED a tune as she approached the double doors to Kincaid Racing.

When Sam had called to ask if she'd meet him in his office, she'd been glad about the unexpected opportunity to spend time with him.

He was waiting as she entered the lobby, his expression forbidding.

"Has something happened to Michael?" she asked, her heart beating wildly.

"No, Michael's in my office."

She exhaled slowly in relief. Her relief was short-lived, though. The set of Sam's shoulders made him seem distant, inaccessible as they walked to his office.

When they entered, he gestured toward the couch in the conversation area, where Michael was sitting in a chair.

"Would you like anything to drink?"

"No, thank you." Tess swallowed hard.

When she sat down, Sam chose the other easy chair.

"Tess, it grieves me to be in this situation. But I think it best if we're all on the same page regarding Michael's future."

Michael leaned forward. "This isn't necessary, Sam. As a matter of fact, I think you're crossing a line because of your relationship with my mother."

Sam smiled icily. "Fortunately, there's no morals clause regarding my behavior. And my relationship with Tess is loving and above reproach."

Michael crossed his arms and grunted. "Yeah, right."

"Tess, you've expressed concerns about Michael's ability to handle the lifestyle that comes with fame. I thought you were simply being overprotective. Now, I find I'm reconsidering. Perhaps I should have considered that you know your son better than anyone."

"What's this all about, Sam? You're scaring me. Is Michael in trouble?"

"Not yet. But if he keeps heading down this road, he might be."

"You're overreacting, man. I haven't done anything other guys my age wouldn't do." Michael's expression was sullen.

"That's open for debate."

"Why do I feel I'm missing something here?" Tess asked.

"Because, against my better judgment, I haven't enlightened you about certain things. Michael got a speeding ticket on Thanksgiving Day. He went to defensive-driving school and I agreed not to tell you."

Tess tried to process the implications. The two men she loved most had been keeping her in the dark. She couldn't begin to express her hurt. And wonder what else they might be keeping from her. "How…disappointing."

"Yes, I knew you would be disappointed. And after the underage-drinking thing, I thought you might drag him back to Phoenix."

"So you withheld information from me?"

"Yes. And I deeply regret it. There are some other things you need to know. Michael has been using the team motor home for…entertaining."

"Parties?"

"No, entertaining of a more intimate nature."

Realization dawned. Tess wanted to cover her ears and pretend she hadn't heard, hadn't understood. But she'd been a single mother too long to shirk the harder duties. And this was definitely one of the hardest.

Turning to Michael, she said, "Since you haven't brought a girl around to meet me, I assume this is a casual fling."

He shrugged. "I hooked up a couple times."

"With the same girl or different women?" She held up her hand. "No, wait, I don't want to know. It's risky behavior either way. And so disrespectful to Sam. How could you do something so…smarmy…after Sam has been so good to you, entrusted you with the motor home and your own condo?"

"Mom, now you're overreacting. I'm a consenting adult, I work hard, win races. I should be able to have a social life without you and Sam acting like I'd committed murder."

Tess wished there was some way to get through to her son. "It's not just the 'hooking up,' Michael. It's the whole series of potentially dangerous behaviors—underage drinking, breaking traffic laws. This has to stop."

"You're not a shrink, Mom. Your baby boy has grown up and you can't handle that I'm making my own decisions."

"No, I can't handle that you're making the *wrong* decisions."

"Maybe if you'd get your own life, you wouldn't be so concerned with what I do." Michael rose and stalked out of the office, slamming the door behind him.

"That certainly went well," Sam commented.

She shook her head slowly. "I can't believe his attitude. It's like I don't even know him. All of the sudden, he's become like his father."

Sam came and sat next to her on the love seat. "I owe you an apology, Tess. A couple, actually. I'm deeply sorry for keeping the speeding ticket from you. You deserved to have that information."

She nodded dully. "He's technically an adult. It was a judgment call. But it does make me wonder what else you might be keeping from me."

"Tess, this is it. I knew it was a bad idea, but I did it anyway, rationalizing that it would save you grief."

"Like my ex rationalized that I didn't need to know our marriage was over until he was out of the country?"

"It's not the same."

"No, but if you feel this way about the smaller things, how can I trust you with the bigger things?"

He grasped her hands. "You can trust me, Tess. I'd never do anything to intentionally hurt you."

She wanted to believe him. But history told her she was too trusting sometimes. "All I can say is that I'll try to get past this."

"We *will* get past this, Tess." He squeezed her hands. "I should also apologize for not taking your initial arguments seriously. I thought Michael had such a good head on his shoulders, he'd have no problem handling racing. Too bad I didn't realize that it would be fame and freedom that would trip him up."

She squeezed his hands in return. "Thank you for admitting you made a mistake."

"I still think Michael's got a phenomenal talent. He loves to race—that much is obvious. But maybe you were right—maybe he needs seasoning first. Do you want me to rescind the contract based on the morals clause?"

Drawing a breath, Tess wished for once not to have a choice. She had the power to maneuver Michael into accepting his fate at Stanford. Yet, she hesitated. "You've just handed me what I wanted so badly for years, what I thought was best for my son. I have to admit, I'm not so sure anymore."

Sam smiled. "Be careful what you wish for?"

"In spades." She hesitated. "Why don't we wait a couple days, see if any of this sinks in. He's scheduled to race this weekend, isn't he?"

"Yes."

"Let's reevaluate after that. If he's had a change of heart, it should be evident. If he hasn't, then Stanford still wants him, though I wonder if he's even mature enough to handle college life."

Chuckling, Sam said, "I have the feeling his present mindset is pretty much a requirement for college. At least from what I've heard."

"You're right about one thing. We *will* get past this." Tess kissed him on the cheek, determined to give their relationship every chance at succeeding. "You're a good man, Sam Kincaid."

"I hope you still think so when all is said and done."

CHAPTER TWENTY

"HEY, MOM, HAVE YOU got a minute?"

Tess glanced up from her needlework, using the remote to turn down the volume on the TV. "Always, Michael."

"I've been thinking about what you and Sam said the other night. I guess I've been acting like kind of a jerk."

"It shows maturity to admit that. What do you intend to do about it?"

"I guess I let things go to my head. I got caught up in my own ego. It's kind of wild, hearing those crowds cheering for me. Having all these girls who wouldn't have given me a second look in high school suddenly thinking I'm pretty great."

"I can see where that could sway even the most grounded man. Have you learned anything from it?"

"I'm still the same guy I was before NASCAR. I probably don't have to say yes to all the stuff that seems to be coming my way now."

"Ah, resisting temptation. I'd like to be able to tell you it gets easier, but the truth is, there will always be temptations to resist. You're learning some important skills."

"So why can't I have some fun and still be a top driver?"

"I guess it depends on how you define fun. The kind you are experimenting with is destructive and dangerous."

"Okay, no need to lecture. I got the point the other day. How do I convince Sam to keep me on?"

"Now I see the reason for this heart-to-heart talk. You're hoping I'll intercede on your behalf. Looks like we should add manipulation to the list of skills you've recently learned."

"Could you talk to him?"

In the past, Tess wouldn't have hesitated to go to bat for her son. But she was starting to understand she hadn't been doing him any favors. "You're an intelligent adult. I'm sure you'll find a way to convince him." She patted his hand. "Remember, actions speak louder than words."

Michael nodded. "You're right. I really want this, Mom. I got sidetracked by some stupid stuff, but I intend to show you and Sam how serious I am."

Tess nodded. "I'm glad to hear it. I want to make sure there's no misunderstanding between us. And remember, intimacy is a beautiful thing. Just make sure you make love for the right reasons."

"Okay, Mom. I've got it now."

She smiled. He wasn't any more receptive to her sex talks now than he had been at ten, thirteen and sixteen. She'd had to try, though.

"YOU'RE SURE you wouldn't rather be down in the pits?" Sam asked, pacing the length of the buffet table in the VIP suite.

"Positive."

"But he might need us to reinforce how important this race is. Make sure his head is in the right place."

Tess touched his arm. "Didn't we discuss this last night? He's an adult and he's responsible for his own decisions. He says he's done with the stupid stuff."

Sam sighed. "I know. But there's a lot riding on this race. Riding on him. It's not like I want to cut him loose."

"You're sounding like an overprotective father. Don't make me tell Ron," she teased.

"I know, I know. Michael can make his own choices and suffer any consequences."

"Exactly."

"How can you be so calm?"

"I'm not. Inside I'm a nervous wreck. But I've got to have confidence in Michael. That he can handle what life throws at him."

"What if I was wrong? What if he can't maintain under pressure?"

Tess rose, putting her arms around him. "Get a grip, Sam. It'll be fine. Whatever happens, it'll be fine."

His smile was sheepish. "I guess I do sound kind of like an overprotective parent."

Fortunately, the race began shortly thereafter—otherwise Tess would have been afraid Sam might wear a path in the carpet from pacing.

Michael started from a decent position and soon moved up to fourth.

Tess cheered wildly. Sam joined her.

Michael drove hard but smart, not taking unnecessary risks. He inched his way up to third place. There were several near misses and one wreck, but he managed to avoid them all.

"If he can hold this position, drafting on the second-place car, he can shoot around one and two when we're down to the last few laps."

And that's exactly what Michael did. He battled it out for second place and succeeded in wresting it away from a top, experienced driver—one who drove both NASCAR Busch Series and NASCAR NEXTEL Cup Series.

Then they were down to the last two laps. Michael went high, trying to pass, but the first car managed to hold him off.

In the next turn, the first-place driver anticipated he'd go high again. Michael went low in a gutsy move, trying to force his way by. Unfortunately, he miscalculated, tapping the lead car in the bumper.

The lead car spun and Michael wasn't able to avoid him. The two cars impacted, spun, and the lead car went low, coasting into the infield. The No. 463 car went high. As Michael's car crashed into the wall, Tess watched in horror. The impact seemed deafening, though logically she knew it wasn't that loud.

Sam stood.

Tess jumped up, her actions automatic. Her only thought was to get to her son as soon as possible.

Sam gripped her arm. "Tess, it's not as bad as it looks. The car is designed to do that, keeping the driver safe inside the cockpit."

"I need to see Michael. Make sure he's okay."

"I understand. I'll get us down there." He grasped her hand and led her into the pit area. Cheers went up around them as it was announced that Michael had gotten out of the car unaided. He'd apparently walked away unharmed.

Tess exhaled slowly. The world stopped spinning. "I've never been so scared in my life, Sam."

He wrapped his arms around her, kissing the top of her head. "I know, sweetheart. Neither have I. Come on, we'll meet him at the EMT station."

"I thought they announced that he was fine."

"They did. Purely a precaution."

Sam strode through the crowd, parting the waves of people by the sheer force of his personality.

When they reached the first-aid stand, he said, "This is Michael McIntyre's mother."

Tess stepped forward. "Is he okay?"

"Yes, ma'am, it appears he's fine. We need to thoroughly examine him, though."

"I understand."

"Mom, is that you?" Michael struggled to sit up.

She pushed through the emergency personnel to grasp his hand. "I'm here, honey. You gave me quite a scare."

His eyes were wide. "All I want to do is get out of here."

He tried to swing his legs over the side of the gurney, but the paramedics stopped him. "This'll only take a couple minutes, then you can go."

"Don't leave, Mom."

"I won't."

"I'm here for you too, son," Sam said.

Michael's mouth tightened. "I'm not your son. And after tonight, I'm not your driver."

"We'll talk about this later." Sam jerked his head toward the media, held back by security.

"Hey, Michael," one of them yelled. "What's your impression of the NASCAR Busch Series?"

"Do you think you have what it takes?" another asked.

"Is there a special lady to nurse you back to health?"

He jerked his thumb toward Tess. "Yeah, my mom."

His grin might have seemed cocky to some. But not Tess. She was close enough to see his hands tremble, the panic in his eyes.

He reminded her of the little boy he'd been, hiding his face during the flying monkey scene in *The Wizard Of Oz*. Her instincts told her he'd meant it when he'd told Sam he wouldn't be his driver anymore. She suspected he was seriously thinking of quitting his racing career.

Instead of feeling victorious at the thought, Tess felt uneasy. As if Michael might be denying an important part of himself by giving up.

IT WAS LATE that evening when Sam helped Tess get Michael up the stairs. He was already stiff and sore after sitting out the rest of the race and on the plane ride home.

"You rest up, son, um, Michael."

"You can bet I will." Michael's words were loaded with meaning.

Sam chose to ignore the underlying threat, reminding himself racing was in Michael's blood. There was no way he could turn his back on NASCAR and the opportunities presented by Kincaid Racing. Could he?

"Do you want me to hang around for a while?" Sam asked.

"No, that's not necessary." Tess seemed distracted and distant. As if she were already mentally packing up her son and taking him to Phoenix.

Sam almost panicked at the thought. "Is there anything I can pick up at the drugstore? I have a friend who's a sports trainer. Maybe he'd come over and look at Michael tonight."

"It's very kind of you, but I'll take him to a hospital if I feel he's been injured that badly. I imagine a good night's sleep and an ice pack will do the trick."

He touched Tess's arm. "We'll talk tomorrow, okay?"

"Yes." Her voice was husky with regret.

Sam told himself she wouldn't, *couldn't* just up and leave. "You won't make any decisions without talking to me, will you?"

"I can't guarantee that, Sam. I have to do what is best for my son. Tonight was a painful eye-opener what life was like for the family of a NASCAR driver. I'm not sure I'm strong enough to support Michael in this endeavor anymore."

TESS HAD SAVED the race to her DVR. She sat up till almost dawn watching the accident over and over, almost as if trying to desensitize herself.

But all it did was re-create the fear, the sick dread that she'd allowed Michael to do something dangerous.

"Mom, what're you still doing up?" Michael knuckled sleep from his eyes. "I came out to get a drink and some ibuprofen."

"I couldn't sleep," she said, patting the couch next to her. "Sit down. We'll talk like the old times. Remember when we used to sit up late and watch all those old movies?"

Michael sat next to her, resting his head on her shoulder. "Yeah, we used to sit like this."

Her heart ached with memories of all the nights they'd watched TV together. Until he'd reached fourteen and the cuddling had stopped.

"I think I made a mistake," he murmured.

"Oh?"

"I got all caught up in the glamour of racing. I didn't have a very good idea of what it really meant."

"What are you saying?"

"I want to quit, Mom. I want to go home to Phoenix and enter Stanford."

Tess's heart squeezed. She wanted nothing more than to load up her son and take him home tonight. But she needed to make sure he didn't make a hasty decision. "Why don't you think about it for a couple days? Nothing has to be decided tonight."

"I don't need to think about it. There's just so much other stuff besides the racing. The media, the fans, providing a good example for kids. And then this happens. I had this wild idea that I was so special I wouldn't ever get hit hard. I thought it was all bumper-car kind of stuff."

"It scared you?"

"Yeah. I hate to admit it, though."

"Maybe a good scare was what you needed. You could have been getting overconfident. Now you know you're not bulletproof—maybe you'll drive that much smarter."

"I don't know. All I can think about is that I made this huge mistake. How easy it would be to go home tomorrow and pick up where we left off."

Tess couldn't help but notice how he'd phrased his remark; "...pick up where *we* left off" after a whole lot of "I" statements. Obviously, Stanford had been her choice as much as his.

It was something she needed to think about when she was alone. Trying to keep him from making a rash decision, she said, "Hiding from your problems isn't the answer. Usually, your problems find you anyway. Besides, do you really think you could do that and not regret quitting racing?"

"I'm not sure."

"Why don't you get a good night's sleep and put off making any decisions? The answer will work itself out."

"I guess. I'll see you in the morning."

Tess only hoped the theory held true for her, too.

CHAPTER TWENTY-ONE

SAM KNOCKED on Tess's door, his pulse pounding. This could be one of the most important meetings of his life.

Michael opened the door. "Come in, Sam. Have a seat."

"Is Tess here?"

"No, she's at the food bank. This needs to be between you and me."

"Okay." Sam sat on the couch.

Michael's gaze was level, though he had dark circles under his eyes, as if he hadn't slept well.

"I started this Kincaid Racing thing without my mother and I'll finish it the same way. It's not working out, Sam. I want you to release me from my contract—use the morals clause if you have to."

"You may never race again." Sam raised his hand as Michael opened his mouth to protest. "No, I'm not threatening you. I'm simply telling you the way the racing grapevine works. No matter how hard I might try to keep the reason under wraps, the truth will get out. Or worse, a perversion of the truth. It might bury your career."

"Believe it or not, I've considered that. I've already

noticed how quickly word gets around. I've decided not to race professionally again. I'll play around at a local track on evenings and weekends just to satisfy my need for speed." He smiled sadly. "Otherwise, I'm going to be a freshman at Stanford this fall."

"You're sure there's nothing I can say to change your mind? You are the most naturally gifted driver I have ever seen. And your ability to calculate weather and track conditions and react before even the computers have processed the variables would have been your secret weapon."

"I didn't know you'd noticed. I thought that was my own little secret."

"Oh, you'd be surprised what I notice."

"Like how pretty my mom looks in blue?"

Sam couldn't help but smile. "Among other things."

"What else?"

Sam made a noise of protest.

"No, really. I'm curious."

"When I first met Tess, I didn't like the way she overprotected you. I thought it was intrusive and just a little desperate. But once I got to know her, I realized she was learning new skills just as you were. She was learning to let go—probably one of the hardest things for a parent to get the hang of."

"I suppose."

"Then, when I got to know her better, I noticed her class, her elegance, the way she always stood by her beliefs. And tenacious—that woman can be like a bulldog with a bone." Sam smiled. "Did I ever tell you about her negotiation tactics at an antique store we found off the beaten path?"

"No, neither did she."

Sam went on to regale him with the story. And how amazing he thought Tess was.

"Are you in love with my mother?"

The question shocked him. Not because Michael had asked, but because he'd studiously avoided asking himself the same question.

"I'm...not sure how to answer that."

"Yes or no is usually a good start." Michael's tight smile didn't meet his eyes.

"You don't need to get sarcastic, kid. It's not as easy as you think. Especially when you're my age and have made some pretty dumb mistakes."

"You think falling in love with my mother would be dumb?"

"No, I didn't say that."

"Are you going to ask my mother to marry you?"

"Hell, no." The answer exploded from him before he had time to think. "I mean, there are a lot of things I would need to consider before marrying a second time."

"I much preferred your first answer." Tess's voice came from behind him. "At least you were honest then."

Sam swung around. "Tess, I didn't hear you come in."

"Obviously," she said, her skin pale, fragile almost.

"I didn't mean that whole thing about marriage the way it sounded. I was just so shocked."

"You find the very idea of marrying someone like me shocking?"

He was digging himself deeper with every response. But he couldn't help trying to rectify the situation. "Of course not. It's just that our relationship hasn't progressed to that kind of commitment yet. We both decided to take it slowly."

Her eyes grew bright with moisture. "Maybe there's a reason for that. Maybe my gut is telling me you're not the kind of man to settle down for long."

"I was married for over twenty years."

"That's different. You had children to raise with Candace."

"What's this all about, Tess?"

"Maybe this thing between us isn't working out. I can't seem to trust you."

"Just because I don't want to get married right now doesn't mean we shouldn't continue to see each other. I figured our relationship should have the chance to grow slowly over time. That way, you could get past whatever's holding you back."

Tess tucked her hair behind her ear. "I have too much on my mind right now, Sam. Maybe we should take a break from seeing each other. Take some time to reevaluate."

"I don't want that, Tess. Why are you pushing me away?"

"Then what do you want?"

"To continue like we were."

"I'm not sure that's a good thing. I need time to think."

Michael stepped between them. "Mom, I asked Sam over here to tell him I quit. I'm going back to Phoenix, then I'll start Stanford in the fall."

"Don't jump into anything, Michael. Things might seem different tomorrow or the next day."

"I figured you'd be happy. Besides, I've done nothing but think about it since the race last night. It's no good. I freaked when the car spun and I saw the wall coming up fast. I'll never forget the sound of the impact."

Sam said, "I'm willing to bet that's a fairly normal response. Don't go throwing your career away over something we might be able to work through."

"You don't understand. There are absolutes in science." He crossed his arms over his chest. "It's who I am. Science is such a part of me, I don't have to think about it. Racing is work and no matter how hard I try, I might never get it right."

"A crisis of confidence—"

Michael turned his back on Sam, effectively shutting him out. "Mom, I feel bad for asking you to take time off work and dragging you across the country for nothing."

She touched his cheek. "Oh, it wasn't for nothing. I've learned so much. Met new people." She glanced at Sam. "I've seen new things. Most of all, I learned that you're a grown-up, able to make your own mistakes and face up to the consequences."

"We'll go back to Phoenix. Back to the way we'd planned for it to be."

Defeat washed over Sam.

Tess's expression was grim when she said, "Yes, we'll go home. I'm sorry, Sam. I really would have liked for things to work out differently."

"Wait—"

"We've already said everything that needs to be said."

"You can't just leave like this."

She stepped forward and grasped his hand in both of hers. "Thank you for the opportunity to come to Charlotte. Thank you for being…my friend. I'll always treasure my memories of our time here."

Sam wanted to drop to one knee and propose. But it would be an empty gesture if neither of them was sure where they were headed.

"Is this goodbye?" His voice was husky.

"Yes, I think it is. Goodbye, Sam." She withdrew her hand from his and turned her back, while Michael escorted him to the door.

A sense of unreality settled in, as if it all were a very bad dream. He only hoped he woke up soon, because losing Tess and Michael hurt like hell.

TESS WAS AMAZED she remained dry eyed as the plane taxied down the runway. Because it felt as if her heart were being ripped out of her chest.

Leaning back in the seat, she closed her eyes and breathed deeply.

"Nervous flier?" the guy next to her asked.

She didn't bother to open her eyes. "Something like that."

More like feeling as if her lifeline had been severed. How had it happened? Somehow she'd created a life in Charlotte. What had been intended to be temporary had begun to seem permanent. And she'd liked it. For the first time in a long time, she'd actually felt like a participant in life, not just doing what she was supposed to.

"Are you okay?" Michael asked.

She did open her eyes for him. And forced a smile when she saw his concerned frown. "I'm fine. Really."

"You don't know how bad I feel about this. If I hadn't insisted on the whole Kincaid Racing thing, we wouldn't have gone to Charlotte and you wouldn't have gotten your heart broken."

"Shh," she gently remonstrated. "I'll recover. I'm an adult. I knew I was letting myself care too much."

"You once told me not to be afraid of caring. That we all were meant to love each other."

Her heart squeezed at his words. Why did he have to remember things she'd told him only when they ran counter to what she now felt? It must be a cruel irony of parenthood.

"Unfortunately, people don't always love us back the way we love them."

"Are you talking about Dad, or Sam?"

Oh, Lord, she'd almost forgotten Michael's father and how it appeared history seemed to be repeating itself. She seemed destined to be the one left behind. Only this time, the love of her life was deserting her, not to find adventure and his dream, but because he simply didn't care enough. The knowledge was so much more painful. But better now than later, once her emotions were one hundred percent engaged.

"Both, I guess. Now, enough questions. Unless you want to reciprocate and tell me more about the 'entertaining' you were doing in the motor home."

Michael placed his MP3 player headphones on his ears and winked. "Got it, loud and clear."

Somehow, Tess didn't think it was the music he talked about.

SAM FOUND Ron in the garage, checking under the hood of the No. 463 car. He wiped his hands on a towel and shut the hood.

"What brings you down here, boss?" Ron asked.

"I thought you might have some suggestions about who we could get to replace Michael."

Ron held his gaze. "I have some suggestions, but I don't think you'll like them."

"Such as?"

"Get your head out of your posterior and convince the kid to come back. And while you're at it, pick up something for his mom—like a ring."

"You know I could fire you for insubordination."

Ron grinned. "You could. But you won't."

"You're very sure of that?"

"Positive. I'm the best and you know it. Besides, I'm only telling you what you already know."

"You think I should bribe Tess with baubles to get to Michael?"

"Tess doesn't impress me as the kind of woman to be bribed. As a matter of fact, she'd probably rip your head off and serve it back to you on a platter if you tried. All very calmly and politely."

"Uh-oh, is that admiration I hear in your voice?"

"Could be. I have to admit at first she reminded me of my ex-wife. I thought she was one of those clingy-type women who wouldn't let a man breathe—whether it was a husband or son. But I realized pretty quick she really wanted what was best for the kid, just didn't quite know it was time to let go. So I helped her."

"You were very hard on her."

"Had to be. Haven't you ever heard of tough love?"

"Sure, who hasn't?"

"Well, she just gave you a walloping dose of tough love. A civilized kick in the pants."

"Hey, she ran, not me." The need to defend himself rankled.

"She ran because you didn't give her reason to stay."

"Is there *anything* around this town that isn't open knowledge?"

"Nope."

"You're enjoying this, aren't you?"

"You bet. It's not often I get to see my esteemed boss at a loss."

"I suppose you know exactly what I should do?"

"Yep."

"Are you going to enlighten me, Ron?"

"Nope. You'll figure it out on your own. Just like you'll figure out a way to get Michael back where he belongs—in the cockpit of that car."

Ron tossed the shop towel in the bin, making a perfect three points. He grinned, winked and walked out the door.

Sam could have sworn he heard a chuckle as the crew chief left.

"I really need to fire him," he muttered under his breath. The problem was, Ron was right.

CHAPTER TWENTY-TWO

THREE WEEKS LATER, Michael tried to get excited about the whole Stanford thing, but he felt as if he was only going through the motions. Worse yet, he felt as if his mother was going through the motions, too.

"That's really great they're going to accept your application," Tess said. Her voice lacked the enthusiasm she'd once had.

"Yeah, it is." He kicked off his shoes and reclined on the sofa. Home again. Safe. Familiar. After a tedious weekend spent at Stanford.

"And that tour they gave of the campus, science department and lab facilities. You liked what you saw?"

"Sure. What's not to like?"

"The people, they seemed friendly?"

"Yes." Especially once one of the group recognized him as being the Michael McIntyre with the short-lived NASCAR career. Several California cuties had given him their phone numbers after that.

His mom sat down and sighed. She'd been sighing a lot lately, but he was pretty sure she didn't realize it. Just as she didn't realize she stared off into space quite a bit. He'd even thought he heard her crying in her room.

She commented, "I'll ask for the time off at work to take you up there when the fall session starts. My boss seems to be glad I'm finally back."

"Mom, do you mind if I ask you a question?"

"Ask away."

"Are you happy to be back?"

She seemed to choose her words carefully. "I'm happy to be on familiar turf. I've stepped right back into my job as if I never left."

"Does it seem sometimes like it was just a dream?"

Smiling sadly, she said, "Yes, it does. Just when I thought it might be a more permanent thing. Are you still doing okay with your decision?"

"Sure. I knew it was for the best." Boy, was that a load of bull. He missed driving like crazy. Dreamed about it at night, and not the nightmares he'd expected after the wreck. No, these were dreams of himself flying, effortlessly in a perfectly set up car, zooming past everyone on the track. The crowd cheered; his heart swelled.

It made science seem a whole lot less interesting than he remembered.

"Have you talked to Sam?" he asked.

"No. I've picked up the phone a couple times, but really what would be the use?"

"Compromise. Getting things out in the open. Getting past whatever it is that's scaring you."

"I'm not scared."

"Yes, you are. And I've never seen you like that before. We've been through some tough times, but you always handled things head-on."

"I...I miss him like crazy." Her eyes filled with tears. "But there's something that holds me back. I really started falling for him, then you're right, I got scared."

He shifted in his chair, his conscience nagging. He'd been selfish, ignoring his mom's happiness to keep things comfortable. "I know I was a jerk about you and Sam. Part of it was because you haven't dated seriously in a long time. I, um, didn't want things to change."

"That's usually my excuse."

"Change happens, Mom. And you did seem really happy with Sam. Maybe you're afraid he'll leave you like Dad did."

She stiffened, frowning. "I don't think—"

"It's okay, Mom. It's not my business."

Clearing her throat, she asked, "How about you? Fess up."

"I don't miss Sam like crazy," he teased. "He was an okay guy. But I do miss the track and my crew, even Ron. He was tough at first, but never asked more than he thought I could give."

Her eyes widened. "That's a mature observation. And very perceptive."

He shrugged. "I have to admit, the college crowd seems kind of, well, immature, now that I've been out in the real world. Well, the NASCAR world."

"Do you think we were too hasty?"

Michael thought back to the wreck and told himself he'd done the right thing. Daydreaming about what-ifs was one thing, actually considering racing at that level again another.

"No. It was the right decision for me." He hoped.

"Yeah, me, too." Her voice lacked conviction. And her eyes definitely lacked that sparkle they'd had when Sam was around. It was tough watching her give up that kind of joy in her life. Sam had been a good guy, all in all, if Michael had just given him more of a chance.

SAM HAD NO CLUE why he was wandering through antique stores on one of his few Saturdays in town. Somehow it simply seemed reassuring. As if Tess might walk through the doors and start bartering with a shop owner.

Maneuvering his way through the crowded store, Sam spied something on a sideboard that didn't seem to fit. Stepping closer, his pulse accelerated. Tucked inside an antique mixing bowl was an old baseball glove. The leather was still supple—someone had obviously oiled it over the years. His eyes widened when he spread it open to look at the palm. It was autographed by one of his favorite Cubs players.

He felt it was significant that he'd found this glove, today, in this place. He had to have it.

The manager must have noticed his interest, because he came over. "May I help you with something?"

Sam tried to feign mild interest. "This seems kind of cool. What do you want for it?"

The manager quoted him a price that made him raise an eyebrow. What would Tess do?

"It's cool, but not that cool." He placed it where he found it, forcing himself not to look back longingly. "Thank you for your time."

As he headed for the door, the manager called, "Wait. I might be able to come down on the price."

This was where Tess would have gone in for the kill. He copied the strategy he'd observed her use time and again—not so different from negotiating commercial real-estate transactions. It worked for him, too, though he suspected Tess would have hammered out a better deal.

He left the shop with the mitt nestled in a clear plastic display box and a shopping bag. Whistling a tune, he couldn't wait to see Tess's expression when he showed her his find.

Then he stopped in his tracks. Tess wasn't there to share the small, secret moments like these. Or the really big things in life, like grandchildren and retirement plans. And the medium stuff in between.

"Sit," Tess commanded, arms crossed over her chest.

"I'm not a dog, Mom."

She inclined her head, like a queen acknowledging the village idiot. Uh-oh, she was in royal-decree mode. That meant he was going to have to do something he didn't want to do. But royal-decree mode meant she'd keep at him until he gave in. It could be hours, days, weeks or months—it all depended on how long he could hold out.

Michael swallowed hard. "What's up?"

"I've done you a terrible disservice."

"How's that?"

"Your father's risk taking scared me, and I apparently passed on that fear to you. Not intentionally, but by stressing how much I valued safety and reliability."

"Hey, Mom, you've always been there for me."

"And I always will be, if I'm able." She glanced down at her hands. "I'm not very proud of what I've done. I ignored your father's good qualities and focused on the bad when I made decisions about your activities. I must've unwittingly steered you to the more cerebral interests, avoiding those I considered risky."

"The peewee-football fiasco was pretty blatant," he teased.

"Please, Michael, this is very difficult for me." She took a deep breath. "I've taught you to be a quitter."

"Say what?"

"A quitter. You were so unaccustomed to physical roughhousing and the daring things guys tend to do, you folded the first time things got really tough."

"Do I need to point out that I crashed into a wall at 180 miles per hour?"

She waved her hand. "No need. I was there, remember? You walked away from it unhurt. Sam took great pains to teach me all the safety measures. You did all sorts of evasive training. But in that instant, my faith failed and it was like being on the sidelines of a peewee football game again. All I could think of was making sure you were totally safe for the rest of your life."

"It's probably a mom thing," he mumbled. This side of his mother made him uncomfortable. It was like a nun wanting to lead a SWAT team.

"No, it was me trying to make sure you didn't grow up to be your father's son. I was not going to stand by and watch you put yourself in danger to assuage some thrill-seeking gene I didn't understand."

"Is there a point to this?"

She stopped, placed her hands on her hips. "The point is that I'm a coward and you were born to—"

The sound of the doorbell interrupted midrevelation. Michael sighed in exasperation.

"Would you get that, Michael, and tell them we don't want to buy any more magazine subscriptions? Maybe I can gather my thoughts and make some sense."

Michael opened the door. Talk about surprises. "Sam."

"Hi, Michael, is your mother here?"

"Um, yeah, come on in."

Sam stepped inside.

Michael watched his mom as she realized it was Sam. Her face lit in a way that was totally awesome. "Sam," she breathed.

"Hi, Tess, I hope you don't mind that I stopped by without calling."

"No, not at all. Is something wrong? Has something happened?"

"No. Well, kind of. I have this for you." He held out a gift-wrapped package.

Michael shook his head in disappointment. The box was too big to contain an engagement ring. Which is what he figured would make his mom totally happy.

"Thank you. Your timing couldn't have been better. We were discussing racing and my lack of courage, both of which involve you. I'd like to complete the discussion before I open your thoughtful gift. Please sit down." Tess gestured toward the couch.

Michael took his place on the couch. Sam sat at the other end.

"Michael, I'll make it short and sweet. You chickened out on racing. That crash shook your confidence and you ran home, where things come easy to you. Well, I'm here to tell you, most of the important things in life involve struggle and sacrifice. A wise man once suggested that a person needs to do what makes him look forward to the day. Even if there are some risks. Even if you have to go out of your comfort zone."

"Now you *are* sounding like Dad."

"The wise man was Sam. But you're right, your father's always lived life to the fullest, no regrets. You don't have a wife and family, so you have an advantage he didn't. And you're wimping out because it got tough."

"Let me get this straight. It scares you when I race because you're afraid for my safety, but you're challenging me to do it anyway?"

"Absolutely. If you don't try, and I mean really try, pulling out all the stops, giving it your absolute all, you'll regret it someday. I can hold my breath now and then during a race if it means you have a shot to figure out whether this is the life you were meant to live."

Michael hesitated. "I'm…scared. This is such a huge thing and if I fail, I fail in front of millions of people."

She stepped close, touching his shoulder. "That's why it takes a special kind of courage to get out there and risk it anyway. You have that courage, Michael."

How could he say no, when his mom put it that way? A tiny spark of hope ignited.

Turning to Sam, he asked, "What do you think?"

Sam shook his head. "No way, you're not drawing

me into this one. You need to decide and then we'll talk."

"What's your heart tell you, Michael?" his mother asked. "What does your gut say?"

Slowly, he smiled. "They both say I should go for it."

She wrapped her arms around him and rested her cheek against his chest. "I'm so proud of you. I love you."

"I love you, too, Mom." He hugged her for a few seconds, then released her. "I've got an errand I need to run. If I'm not mistaken, this guy flew thousands of miles to talk to you. Oh, and Mom—you've got a lot more courage than you give yourself credit for."

TESS ALMOST WISHED Michael would have stayed, easing the strain of seeing Sam again. She allowed herself the luxury of drinking in his presence while she fiddled with the wrapping paper on the box.

He cleared his throat. "I'm glad to see you."

"It's been a long three weeks."

"The longest. Are you going to open that?" He nodded toward the gift.

"Of course." Had it been a smaller box, she might have gotten weak in the knees, thinking it contained an engagement ring. As it was, it could be almost anything.

Removing the wrapping paper, Tess smiled, bemused. "A baseball glove…with the ball we bought."

"Not just any glove. It's autographed, too. It's the same year as the ball—the year I would have been starting shortstop if everything had gone according to plan."

She smiled. "Your dream?"

"Yes. I found this glove in a little antique store. I went out antiquing just so I could feel close to you. And when I found the mitt, it just seemed so prophetic."

"I'm not following."

"You and I are opposites in some ways. You like things predictable and safe; I like to shake things up every once in a while. You were looking for permanence in our relationship and I wasn't ready yet."

"Is there a point?"

"The ball and glove have totally different functions. The glove is there to catch the ball when it hurtles through space. Can't have a game without both a ball and glove. Equally important, though nothing alike?"

It had been a long day and Tess didn't like the way he danced around the subject. "Do me a favor, Sam, leave out the baseball metaphors. I don't understand what you're getting at."

"I guess what I'm saying is that I don't want what we have to be over. You and I fit together perfectly. It's about time I started taking risks where they really count."

Tess blinked. She was almost afraid to hope he meant what she thought he meant. Still, she stepped closer.

He met her halfway and grasped her hands in his. "Tess, I love you with my whole heart. And I'm willing to do whatever it takes to make you feel secure in our relationship."

Her eyes misted, and her mouth wobbled. His absolute sincerity soothed her wounded ego. "I've loved you for a long time now, Sam. You shouldn't have to prove yourself to me. I know you're an honorable man. And I love that you bring spontaneity and daring into my life. It's my old stuff getting in the way, making me afraid you'll leave like Michael's father...."

Sam wrapped his arms around her and drew her close. It felt so right to be held by him. Safe, secure, yet exciting.

Stepping back, he reached into his pants pocket and withdrew a lovely velvet box. Small and square, it could only be one thing. Or so she hoped.

Sam pressed the box into her palm. "Will you marry me, Tess, in spite of my crummy baseball metaphors? Even though it took me a while to get it right where we're concerned?"

"You get the important things right, Sam Kincaid. Of course I'll marry you. As long as you promise to set me back on the right track if I start getting afraid."

He wrapped his arms around her and held her close again. She could hear his heart thud beneath her ear as she rested her head against his chest.

"You've got a deal, lady."

EPILOGUE

Next season

MICHAEL MCINTYRE WAS on the last fifty laps of possibly the most important race of his career. He needed to finish third or better to stay in contention for the Chase for the NASCAR NEXTEL Cup. That meant he could race with the best of the best.

His current position on the track was sixth. Normally, there wouldn't have been a decision involved. He would race with balls to the wall and not back down till he had at least third place.

But this was the track where he'd wrecked so badly. And though he'd never admit it to anyone, it was the track that made him sweat. He had avoided it—until now.

His hands flexed on the steering wheel. He could do this.

He waited for his chance. The fifth-place car held its line on the low side. Michael went high and got around it. He tried the same move several laps later with the fourth-place car, but the veteran driver either had a terrific spotter or he'd seen the No. 463 car coming.

Because he blocked Michael at the turn. And the next turn. And the next.

Sweat pooled inside Michael's uniform.

"What's going on, kid?" Ron's voice came over his headset.

"Can't get around him."

"*Can't* never did anything, son."

"Easy for you to say, old man. He won't let me by."

"Then you make your own path."

"Yeah, sure. I remember the last time I did that at this track." Michael hoped he kept the fear out of his voice.

"You can do this. You're strong and smart. Use that genius brain of yours and outthink him."

"Will do." Michael smiled grimly.

He got right on the guy's bumper, crowding him for all he was worth, hoping he'd rattle him enough to make a mistake. But not so much that they both wrecked big-time.

The veteran driver didn't give an inch.

Outthink him.

Michael formulated a plan. It was gutsy. Some might even call it insane. But if his calculations were right, he might pull it off. And if he was wrong...

His courage faltered. He could hear the impact, see the pieces flying into the air. Smell burning plastic. Feel the heat.

He couldn't do this. Fourth place would have to do.

No way.

His mom had risked everything for him. She'd shown him the courage it took to be a single mom and fight for him. She'd taken chances of her own when past experience told her she might not win. She'd pushed Michael back into racing and married Sam Kincaid. And now Michael was big brother to a sweet little thing from China. How much courage did that take, when both Mom and Sam thought they were through raising kids?

All he had to do was get around one lousy car.

Michael concentrated on his plan. Waiting. Hoping he was right.

The wind shifted as they approached turn two. Michael was prepared for it and adjusted the force he used turning the wheel.

The third-place car didn't account for the change and pushed to the outside in the turn. Michael was barely able to squeeze by on the inside. He whooped for the sheer joy of it as he took a solid third place.

Later, Michael was interviewed in his hauler by one of the national sports shows. His mom, Sam and his baby sister, Leanne, were seated off to the side.

"That was one gutsy move you used to take third place," the commentator said. "Where'd you learn that?"

He smiled slowly. "From my mom, who taught me there are some chances worth taking."

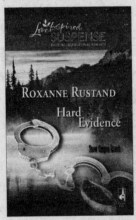

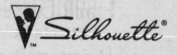

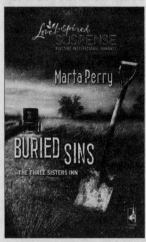